Fae'd Up and Frustrated - Book 4

ANNA DARE

Le Rue Publishing
320 South Boston Avenue, Suite 1030
Tulsa, OK 74103
www.LeRuePublishing.com

ISBN: 978-1-7335960-6-0

To Chunky Monkey.

To Chunky Monkey.

"Baby-napping! Our first case is a baby-napping!" Seena's jaw drops as he stares down at our 'team assignment' folder. We're two months into our training at the Tres Lunas Police Academy, and we now have our first, official off-campus case of our own. (Obviously, we'll have a supervisor with us.) But hell-to-the-yeah! We get to test our skills and see how we do.

From the cubicle on our left, I can hear another recruit groan. "Trolls," a vamp named Petey whines. "That stinks."

All around us, the chatter starts up as different recruits get their first team assignments. There's a feeling of anticipation and dread in the air. It's kind of like the moment on your birthday, right before you open that present from your grandmother—not the one who gives you super soakers and fun stuff, the grandma who hasn't heard that children don't appreciate books on manners and embroidered handkerchiefs.

Seena shakes his black head of hair as he scans the first page of our assignment. "Hell no! They want us to find people who stole babies? I thought we were supposed to get low-level shit!"

I turn in shock to stare at Seena Mostafavipour, my miniature-Arabian-horse shifter partner who (ironically) is Persian. His hair is a mess, and he straightens his glasses as he re-reads the file, as if that will change the words on the page.

"Hold up." I raise my hand. "Wait. You think this case is about what?" I push back my rolling chair so I can get a better look at him. We're crammed into a tiny cubicle stuffed with two desks and two chairs in a space that's really meant for one, so I can't back up much. (Tres goes all out for its trainees. Our cubes are the lap of luxury.)

Seena cocks his head and looks at me like I'm ridiculous. He yanks at his scratchy police uniform collar as he repeats, nice and slow for me, "Baby-napping."

"Yeah, but you said—"

"The kidnapping of infant children. A crime that's just about the worst thing—"

"Whoa, whoa, who-o-oa!" I can't help dragging out the word as if I were directing a horse. You know, because he's a horse shifter. (What? He messes with me all the time. He totally played that stupid 'What Does the Fox Say' song during workouts last week.) "Seena, are you telling me that in LA, people *actually* kidnap babies?"

Seena transferred to Tres Lunas from LAPD. And he's still working on the mental transition from an all human police force to an all supernatural one. Tres Lunas is the only completely supernatural town in Southern California. And I'm so glad Seena moved here. He's my bestest bud at the Academy.

"Um. Yes. People kidnap babies all the time," Seena says.

I close my blue eyes and try to picture it. My dad was human. I was raised human when I was a kid, but after dad died, I was taken in by magicals and I've lived in Tres for so long, that sometimes I forget about the outside world. The human world. "So, there are people out there that steal babies. But ... all they do is scream and poop!"

I open my eyes to find Seena staring at me. "Yeah, so?"

"So, who in their right mind would wanna steal a baby?"

"Why is this a foreign concept for you?" he wrinkles his brow.

I pull a hair tie off my wrist and toss my blonde hair up into a ponytail. "Maybe because someone would be nuts to try to steal a shifter baby. They'd be sniffed out in half a second. Fae already hand their kids out to others like candy, so that wouldn't be a thing. I mean, and really, who could stand a troll baby? Think of the smell!"

Seena waves the file in his hands. "Then what the hell is this case about?"

I laugh and grab the file from him. "Who put rocks in your oatmeal this evening? Geez. Look, right there. Baby-napping is an addiction. To a drug." I grab the file, flip a sheet of paper and point. Of course, I'm more familiar with the file layouts than Seena is, so I know exactly where to look. I used to be a paralegal before I started training to be a cop.

"What?"

I sigh and try to think of the human equivalent. "It's kinda like ... I think humans call it hero? That drug that makes people all chill?"

"Heroine?"

"Oh, yeah. The girl one."

"Baby-napping is a drug?"

"Well, that's not the name of the drug. The drug is actually Nappies. But that's the addiction, right? Baby-napping. Who doesn't wanna sleep like a baby?"

Seena rubs his forehead and sighs. "Okay. Drug addicts. I guess that's better than stolen babies. So, this drug just makes people fall asleep?"

I laugh. "Heck no! You need to read the whole file next time, Black Beauty. It turns them *into* babies."

"What!!?" Seena rubs a hand over his jaw. "Now I'm picturing babies in plaid shirts sitting in cardboard boxes in back alleyways that are full of broken glass and overflowing dumpsters—"

I laugh. "Dude! Lay off the crime shows. Geez. They aren't outside. They have nap shacks."

He scrunches his forehead in confusion.

"Like ... you know, geez ... I need to Goblin this. I dunno enough about the human drug world." I drag out my phone and use the supernatural search engine for a few seconds. I also shoot off a text asking my boyfriend, Luke, if he knows about any drug shack places back when he was alive. (Luke is the world's hottest, Viking-god-wannabe vampire. And he's mine. All mine. Since last week, anyway.)

Before Goblin can spit out an answer that's not full of random click bait, Luke gets back to me.

"Opium dens," I read the text out loud. "Not sure what that is. But Luke says that's what nap shacks are like. Did they have cribs and cages for opium people to sleep in?" I look up at

Seena, who's flipping through our case file and muttering to himself.

"What? Huh? Not sure—" Seena's answer gets cut off as our oh-so-awesome boss approaches.

Diego Flores leans on the edge of our cubicle, giving us a death glare.

I glance side to side, trying to figure out why the tiger shifter is angry at us. "We didn't do anything—"

Flores, aka Flowers on the force—nicknamed for his kind, beautiful personality (hear the sarcasm there?)—rolls his eyes. "I'm supervising your dumb asses on this one. So, let's get a move on."

My shoulders immediately slump. Flowers and I don't see eye to eye on much. And that's not just because I'm a five-foot-four, wingless part-fae and he's a six-foot-plus Hispanic athlete whose toe muscles probably give him an extra inch in height. Nope. Flowers is what you'd call a disciplinarian.

Discipline and I ... we're not like BFFs. JR is my BFF and she's totally not a disciplinarian. She's part nymph—wilds and woodlands and all that.

The disciplinarian is staring at me all grouchy-like. As if he can understand my wandering thoughts. Thank frickin' goodness he can't. Because when he's around, they're pretty grumptacular.

Seena pops out of his seat and grabs his coat. I sigh as I grab my jacket and follow the two down to the parking garage that houses our police vehicles.

I was hoping a mummy named Darrell would be our supervising officer for this assignment. He seemed pretty cool on the last case I worked. But I guess he hasn't recovered from that cat attack a few days ago. I heard he had a couple loose threads when he walked through the station. Bad timing, because someone had brought in some cat shifters high on catnip. I play out the whole incident in my mind, imagining them batting at him and getting tangled up in his bandages. I smother a laugh as I climb into the backseat of the car, letting Seena ride shotgun.

He and Flowers talk about drug crime stats in Tres Lunas. They're going over boring things like the illegal use of Ironmen, a testosterone and iron mixture that shifters love to use in the FFA, Fae Fighting Arts. The drug makes athletes kick serious fae ass due to the iron, but the iron also kicks the taker's ass. As in, they end up shitting iron. Which is not worth it, IMHO. But what do I know? I think voluntary exercise is dumber than most trolls. And that doesn't even cover voluntary fighting.

"New topic!" I announce. "I don't need to picture hot guys with metallic shi—" I can't finish the word. My mother, the sweet kind fae that she is, put a cursing curse on me during my teen years, to stop my potty mouth. I still haven't figured out how to lift it. So, I literally cannot say a goddamn curse word aloud. "Excrement," I improvise lamely, using the word to finish my sentence and to curse my mom at the same time.

"What happened to your Persian cursing?" Seena asks me.

"Takes too much thought," I grumble. "The other day I couldn't remember one of the phrases you taught me. Cursing at someone is ineffective when you have a five second pause before you insult them. Obviously ... I mean, look at my statement about metal turds."

Flowers rolls his eyes, "Too much thought is always a problem for you."

"Hey!"

"You should be listening to our conversation to glean as much as you can about different drug effects, seeing as we're on a drug-related case right now." Flowers lectures me as he steers through a lower-class neighborhood.

I consider arguing, but it's too early in the night to get into with him. Instead, I sniff and stare out the window. The houses are double-stacked, meaning the garage apartment behind the main house has been converted into a second house with a full family in it. California real estate is killer expensive. Especially for those of us not on the 'Richest of...' lists. The driveways are full of rusty cars, and the streets are lined with them, too. There are a lot of ghetto gates on the front doors and bars on the windows. I stare sadly at the little kids playing 'tag the shifted kids' in the front yards of those houses. I always feel bad for kiddos when their house kinda looks like a jail. Or a zoo exhibit, which is what the house with the tag-playing flamingo kids looks like.

Flowers parks on the side of the road, near what looks like an abandoned, boarded-up, two-story brick house. The yard is overgrown and full of trash. One of the upstairs windows has a hole in it.

"Are you sure this is the place?" I ask, "I thought Nappies was an expensive drug."

"They are," Flowers responds as he pockets his keys and opens his door.

"Dude. Uh-uh," I make a face and shake my head as Seena helps me out of the car and we both stare up at the creepy house. The brisk November wind hits us just right, making my nose start to leak just as the scent of freshly ruined diapers wafts down from the house. I grab a tissue out of my pocket and wipe and shield my nose. "I think I shoulda' brought a gas mask. Maybe tactical gear."

"Addiction makes people make bad choices," Flowers lectures as he comes around the front of the car. "A lotta shifters get addicted to Nappies. They like the chill at first. But then, they like the mindset; they like forgetting their problems and having someone take care of them. And they get hooked. It becomes an everynight thing. They stop thinking about things like cleanliness—"

Workout addict wants to critique daily addictions? Well then … "Agreed. Addicts also stop using normal chairs or eating normal meals. Instead, they eat nasty things like protein bars and sit on exercise balls—" I retort.

Flowers glares at me. "Or eat jellybeans and sneak naughty books under their desk?"

Damn. He burned me back. I better not read at work for a week. Okay, who am I kidding? I'll go a day at most. Fuck. I am addicted. I glare at Flowers and debate my next words, wondering how far I can take this before I get punished.

Seena glances between the two of us and holds up his hands. "I'm out."

Flowers shakes his head at me one last time before slipping into instructor mode. "I'm going up first. Seena, you go around to cover the back door. Do not go in on your own. We'll come to you. Fox, you got my back?"

I nod. Much as he might annoy the crap outta me, he's a decent cop. And if it comes to him or some junkie, I'll pick the tiger-shifter every time.

"Wait," I grab Flowers' shoulder. "Should I go first?"

"What? No—why?"

"Well, didn't the tiger want to eat Mowgli? Isn't that a thing? Eating babies?"

Flowers' jaw tics. "This isn't a Disney movie."

"Are you sure—"

"Get the hell behind me, Fox," Flowers growls and stomps toward the house.

"Okay, geez. But I don't think our insurance covers attacks on infants."

"It does cover friendly fire."

"Well, shoot. I mean—don't," I mutter.

Flowers doesn't laugh as he approaches the door. His tension makes my heart speed up.

This can't be that dangerous, right? We're walking into a room full of babies.

I hear a high-pitched yowl inside. Someone must have shifted to a baby kitten.

Kittens are so not dangerous. So why is Flowers scared?

He takes a deep breath and braces himself. That makes me feel like I should widen my stance. I mean, I guess a baby elephant shifter could come barreling out. Who takes care of these babies anyway? Oh … now I get why Flowers is tense.

"Tres Lunas Police!" he yells. "We have a warrant."

He looks down at his watch as we wait for a response.

My eyes are glued to the door handle. I think I see it turn. I stiffen. I blink. Nope. Just a stressed-induced hallucination.

Flowers yells again. (Our rulebook says you have to yell twice since shifters mid-shift might need another second to get to the door.)

When there's no answer, Flowers lifts his leg and power kicks that door. He leaves a hole in the middle. He reaches through the hole with one hand and holds onto the handle with the other.

He turns the front knob, opening the door. But … there is no click.

My jaw drops as I stare at him. Did my instructor just make a boo-boo? "Was the door *unlocked*?" I stage-whisper.

"No," he scoffs.

"But I didn't hear the lock click."

He schools his features, which is a definite tell from Flowers. The door was totally unlocked. He shoulda' checked it instead of being a showoff. But why does he think he needs to look like a badass in front of me?

Flowers snaps in my face. "Focus, Fox," he chides.

I press my lips together, ready to follow him in. But I know I'm right. And I'm feeling a bit smug. I'll have to figure out a way to rib him about this. Before I can think of anything, he swings the door open.

We step into a front hall and the first thing we see is an older woman passed out on the floor. Her pale grey curls are matted. She has a flower print apron on. A baby bottle is on the ground near her hand, and it leaks milk onto the wood floor. It looks as if she was carrying it to feed one of the many infants I can hear bawling in a side room.

Flowers gestures for me to approach her. He covers me, stepping around the woman to check the nearby doorways and clear the rooms.

I crouch and put my fingers to the woman's neck.

There's no pulse. Crap.

"She's dead."

2

F lowers clears the rest of the house while I let Seena in through the back door, which is also unlocked. Apparently, security isn't a big deal at this nap shack. Or maybe the locks are just broken. Looks like just about everything else in this house is.

It doesn't make sense to me, though. I mean, if I was a drug dealer, I wouldn't want people to be able to just walk right in and grab my stash. Or maybe it's magically protected. Or maybe clients take the drugs in the backyard. The dead grass out there did look kinda flattened. In which case, if I was the dealer and had to inject clients and then I had to carry a baby inside each and every time, I'd definitely leave the place unlocked. I mean think about it. Baby bear shifters? What if they don't turn into human babies? The data suggests about half of all shifters go animal when this shit's injected.

I shut the door and wipe my hand on my pants. Even the doorknob in this place is filthy. I crinkle my nose. If I was a dealer, I'd have higher cleanliness standards than this, too. Not that I'd ever be a dealer ...

I join Seena and we stand around in the outdated, sticky-looking kitchen, waiting on Flowers. There's a little butcher block island that rolls. On it is a gallon of milk, an empty saucer, and a cutting board with a knife and a bunch of vegetable ends: carrots, celery, lettuce, etc.

I put the back of my finger against the milk carton. It's still cold. I resist the urge to put it back in the fridge.

Seena scolds me, "Dude, this is a possible murder scene."

"I know," I whisper yell. "I just wanted to know how fresh the milk was. I mean, did this woman just die or has it been out awhile?"

Seena shakes his head at me but doesn't scold further. "I can't tell if we have the worst or best luck of any rookies on the force. I mean, what are the chances of us coming here and finding a dead body?"

I shrug. "You're the math guy." Internally, I agree with him. I just wanted to arrest a few doped-up magicals and be done for the night. Not happening now. Even if it ends up this woman died of natural causes, I wouldn't put it past Flowers to have Seena and I practice evidence collection just for kicks.

The cries from the babies in the front room get as loud and shrill as those airhorn thingies sporty people use when they feel like being dickwads to the people sitting next to them. It's awful. I use my hands as earmuffs while Seena and I wait for Flowers to come back and give us the 'all clear.'

Flowers trusts me enough to watch his back when he kicks down a door but not enough to go through a death/potential murder site without contaminating 'every last shiny thing.' His words. So, I stare at Seena, bobbing my head, covering my ears and pretending to listen to *Jeopardy* countdown music as I wait instead of the piercing melody of crying babies.

"Maybe we should call a sitter," Seena grabs my arm and pulls me over to peer into the living room, where there are at least five cribs and two stacks of cages filled with ... I squint.

"Is that a squirrel with a rhino face?" I pull my flashlight off my belt and shine it into one of the cages. It totally is. Curled up on a towel, with his tail brushing his nose horns, the little brown squirrel has two grey ears that fold up like rolled paper, just like a rhino. His head is over-sized. Most baby heads are. But I mean, like, really really over-sized. It's a mini rhino head on a squirrel body. I don't think a squirrel neck could hold that head up. But then, the baby blinks and proves me wrong, lifting his head and snuffling at me, making his horns jerk up and down.

"Weird," Seena whispers.

I pull my flashlight away from the cage as the rhino-squirrel's adorable black eyes blink at me. He yawns and goes back to sleep once the light isn't in his face.

I shine the light at the next cage down, which is quite a bit bigger. Inside, a group of fluffy little yellow chicks huddle together. Their feathers are at that fuzzy stage of adorableness. One turns its tiny face toward me, and I realize it has the face of a puppy dog. The feathers turn to fur somewhere around its forehead and it has a wet little black nose. Pup chicks. Chick pups. Chickie pups. Holy helium balloons! I didn't know such adorableness was possible. Is there anything in the world that's cuter than a baby chicken combined with a baby puppy face? If there is, I haven't frickin' seen it. Cute aggression hits me hard, and the urge to snuggle and squish those little suckers comes on quick. Flowers was probably right not to take me through the house.

I turn off my light, before I wake up any more babies. I take a deep breath to smash down the cute aggression, grip Seena's hand, and yank him back into the kitchen.

"Ow!"

Whoops. Guess I took out some of the need to squish out on Seena. "Sorry, but did you see those chickie pups? I'm dying." I put away my flashlight and bury my hands in my pockets, so I don't accidentally start kneading Seena's arm. "Cuteness overload." I shake my head.

Seena shakes his head too, but because he's disagreeing with me. "It's a damn shame, that's what it is. Those poor shifters."

I furrow my brow. "Did you not see the same thing I just saw? Hecka cute!"

Seena waves a hand at that room. "Yeah, I saw. Did you see the grasshorse?"

"What?"

"Grasshopper horse? Geez. Talk about a nightmare. No wonder these guys are drug addicts."

I squint at Seena.

I go back to the doorway and shine my flashlight around the living room. There are several human babies fussing in cribs. (They are nowhere near as adorable as the chickie pups.) There's a tall empty cage next to the cribs that has a couple feathers stuck in the newspaper lining. Not there. I swing the light around some more. Sure enough, in a tiny cage perched on an end table, a little green shifter has the shape of a horse and tiny black hooves. But the critter's body looks like a tiny, thumb-sized horse was covered in green armor. No horsing around—he looks like a miniature badass. Like if the ants ever have an apocalypse, he'll be the horse that brought it. Grasshorse. Freaking bohemoth of the backyard insects. A movie narrator's voice clicks on in my head as I stare at the miniature guy. "Watch out, black widow. The grasshorse is out for vengeance." I picture the camera zooming on the grasshorse rearing up on its hind legs.

I trudge back into the kitchen and click my light off. "What's wrong with that?" I point back at the cage in the living room. "He might be the most kick-booty, ninja-awesome grasshopper around."

Seena shakes his head. "Not if he was born into a horse family."

"Oh." I finally get it. Yeah. Badass among the ants. Not so much around real horses. Runt of the litter is an understatement.

"My aunt had a seal-horse."

"A sea horse?" I ask, thinking he said it wrong.

"No. A seal-horse. Her son, Duke, has the body of a seal, head of a horse when he shifts. Pretty much ended her marriage since my uncle's pure horse."

"Huh," I'm not really sure what to say. My life pretty much revolved around fae issues growing up. Lotta flying envy. Elemental magic envy. Beauty envy. How about just a lotta envy in general?

Shifter issues sound different. I think about the shifters I know. But most shifters spend their working hours as humans, unless they're like my ex-boss Arnold who likes to shift his lower half to wolf in a disgusting display of animal prowess that's completely office inappropriate.

I've really never contemplated what happens when shifters mix. Most of them in Tres are pretty rigid about not mixing with other shifters. "A seal-horse. How does that happen—"

Seena gives me a *look*.

I backtrack. "I mean, I know how babies are made, doofus. But, like, how does that convo not come up before people do the deed?"

Seena sighs. "In Tres, things are so open. Magical creatures are safe here. But in human cities, a lotta shifters never talk about what they are. Hide it even. They try to avoid shifting if at all possible. Repress it." Seena waves his hands at the front room, "My guess is that a lotta those people in there are the result of one-night stands. Or shifters who thought they were mating with humans, diluting their magical genes … when surprise! They weren't. They mated with another repressed shifter. It's a real problem."

I tilt my head in thought. "But, like, sometimes you get hardcore cool combos like hippogriffs, right?"

Seena sighs and shakes his head at me. "More often, you get a poor animal who can't fit into either side of their family. Duke, my cousin … can't go run through the meadow with the fam. Can't go underwater and use his flippers because his horse head can't handle staying under. He's stuck."

I bite my lip, "What's he do about it?"

Seena shrugs. "He ran off when he turned eighteen."

Sadness smacks me across the face and my cheeks heat up. That's the worst. I didn't fit in, but at least I had my dad. Then Jacob. "Sorry." I'm not sure what else to say. Other than someone always has it worse than you. I kick the memory of my nineteen year-old-self. 'See? You had no reason for a pity party!' I tell her. She flips me off and goes back to putting on black eyeliner.

Seena shrugs and stares at the vegetables on the cutting table. "Hey, is that blood?" He points at the knife.

I circle the island to stand next to him. Sure enough, the knife has a couple drops of blood on it. "Maybe she cut her finger chopping up baby bunny food? The old lady?" I suggest, shrugging.

"Yeah, maybe she got distracted."

"Easy to do here," I say as the crying babies are interrupted by a strange thumping in one of the rooms upstairs. A little bit of dust trickles down from the light fixture overhead. "Crud. I hope there's not a gorilla shifter or something up there pounding on Flowers."

"Should we check?" Seena's hand reaches for his belt, where we trainees are equipped with flashlights and handcuffs. Excellent tools for facing down drug-addled shifters.

"Maybe we should call for backup," I murmur.

Just then, Flowers bursts into the room. "Hippo shifter cage is broken upstairs," he pants. "I called for backup. And the ME. We better move out back."

"You're a tiger!" I tell him.

"HIPPO!" he yells as if that explains everything. I'm about to argue when a loud snort and ungodly wailing sound comes from the floor above.

"Crap," Seena mutters, pulling at his sleeves nervously.

"What's wrong?" I ask.

"Hippos are crazy aggressive," Seena mutters.

"This is a baby," I argue.

Flowers clears his throat. "His dose of Nappies musta' worn off. Because he was getting bigger by the second." He heads toward the back door.

I grab Flowers' sleeve and yank him back. "We can't leave all these babies here!"

I pull him toward the living room and he begrudgingly follows as I grab two cages—strike that, a baby calf is heavy as hell, I set him down and keep the chickie pups—one cage and move toward the back door.

"Hold up!" Seena stops me. "Why don't you just make that hippo get lost?"

I turn to stare at him as a giant body thunders down the stairs, literally causing the walls of the house around us to shake. Baby hippo has reached adult, stair-crushing proportions.

My heart jumps in my throat. "Where?" I ask, eyes flickering between Seena and Flowers.

A thump makes the floorboards shake beneath us like an earthquake. Oh shit.

Flowers grits out, "Anywhere! He's compromising a crime scene!"

"He'll trample random people!" I argue.

But then, suddenly, the hippo's in the doorway. I see a giant set of jaws dropping open. Who knew hippo teeth were as big as my forearm? Holy wrinkled shirtballs. *I'm* about to get trampled. Or eaten. "That hippo's lost in a field with no one around it for miles!" I say as I shake my hands in a wild freak out motion. And fuck! My leg is on fire, I drop the cage of baby chickie pups I was carrying, my uniform pants rip, and my right leg goes chicken. It sprouts feathers and a claw unfurls inside my shoe. I fall to the floor as the hippo disappears and my stupid power works.

"Corn sticks!" I curse as the chickie pups burst out of their broken cage and swarm over my feathered leg. I try not to move because I'm worried that I'll crush the adorable little suckers. They start to nuzzle. I almost feel maternal for a second. Until one of them nips and then I'm backing away and shaking them off like vermin. "Son of a booger butt, puppy teeth are sharp!"

I latch onto Seena and force him to pull me upright, away from the nipping teeth. I sling an arm around his neck so he can help me stumble around the room, but we've hardly made it two feet away from the chickie pups before a human baby's scream rises above all the other chaos. It sounds tortured. Truly tortured. The sound has Seena dragging me toward the cribs. He props me up on the edge of a crib and picks up a little brown-haired baby whose face is red as a tomato. Seena awkwardly pats the baby's back and starts doing this bouncing squat thing, bending his knees. He coos at the kid.

The screaming, thankfully, stops. I've never really been around a lotta kids. But apparently bouncing is good for them.

A group of adult voices trail in from the front yard and I give a sigh of relief. Backup is finally here. Seena turns too, putting his back to me, with that scrunched up little baby face looking at me all weird and judgy over Seena's shoulder.

"Look at this place—" I recognize Bennett's voice. My ex has a hot gravelly voice that I could pick out of a crowd. Unfortunately, I often hear it in a crowd because he's my boss's boss. He's the head of the entire felony investigation department. Bennett French, the big-muscled, black-haired poster-boy for steamy dragon shifters everywhere, steps into the hallway.

And that's the moment the little monster in Seena's arms projectile pukes … right onto my face.

3

I start spitting. Because that shizzle got in my mouth. And while it's not the worst thing I've ever tasted— don't ask—the very fact that I have baby puke in my mouth makes me want to puke.

I gag. I lean over and put my hand on the wall.

"Fox, stop contaminating the possible crime scene!" Flowers yells at me.

I swipe at my mouth with my sleeve. My sleeve comes away covered in white alien slime. Seriously. That's what it looks like.

"I wanna file assault charges," I gasp, shaking my sleeve even as Flowers comes over and grabs my arm to stop me.

"Contamination," he growls again. And then, as if my latest words have just registered, he recoils, "You wanna file charges against a baby?"

I point at the white ooze dripping from my hair. "Do you see this?" His lip curls and I continue, "That's not really a baby. We don't even know if the mental state fully regresses on Nappies. You shoulda' seen how that little guy looked at me. He knew what he was doing. He puked on purpose."

"I can't tell if you're serious."

"Totally serious." Totally fucking with Flowers. But I *am* totally pissed about being covered in baby puke. I hold his eyes as long as I can. But I'm weak. I cave and a tiny smirk crosses my face.

His eyebrows come down. "Not funny. Take it outside if you're gonna yak." He turns away, but not before I see a hint of a grin on his face.

Damn straight. I'm hilarious.

I grumble under my breath but don't actually argue with him. Flowers likes to give out awful punishments for insubordination. "Am I allowed to go clean up?"

He nods.

"Are there spare clothes in the car?"

"You really think I'm gonna let you repeat the bog pants incident?"

Crap. He's never gonna let that go. You lose one borrowed pair of pants into a bog pit on purpose to punish someone … "I bought you new pants."

He just shakes his head.

I turn to Seena. He's putting the growing baby, now the size of a two-year-old, back into its crib. "Seena, please tell me you have spare clothes."

Seena just raises an eyebrow at me when he turns back. "Did you want something with rainbow sparkles or a leather collar?"

I glare at him. "That was an official police undercover op. You should be proud of that moment!"

"You put a poster of that moment up in the women's bathroom!"

"That wasn't me." Technically, I had JR hang up that gorgeous poster featuring Seena's mini-horse self all dolled up like a pegasus. It's been a bathroom hit.

I try not to smile at the memory of him made up like some little girl's plastic pony. It was epic. God, sometimes I love myself so much. But then, I remember, it's this same self who's now screwed out of clean clothes. My self-love deflates a bit. Maybe I should be nicer to my co-workers.

Behind me, I hear a throat clear. Double crap. It's Bennett. I don't turn around. I don't want him to see me like this.

"Fox, you need clothes?"

"Yes, sir," I keep it formal and avoid humiliating eye contact with his deep green eyes. I hate the little part of me that wants to turn to him and blink like some ditz and let him pick me up, carry me out of this hell hole, and solve all my problems. I'm a grown-ass woman. I can solve my own problems by begging co-workers for clothes. Only problem is … my co-workers are dickwads who can't forgive and forget.

I stare at the grasshorse across the room. It's slowly turning human, the arms and legs have shifted and are growing larger. The torso has started to change. I point to let Flowers know he should go take care of that before the shifter breaks the table. He walks over to pull the grasshopper-horse shifter out of his cage and Seena disappears out the front door.

"Zoe?" Behind me, Bennett speaks up.

"Yes?" A bell-like voice rings out.

I cringe. Fuck my luck. Zoe Nightingale, aka every woman's nightmare, is here to witness me covered in baby puke. She's a tall, willowy elf who looks like a supermodel but is actually a medical examiner, which just makes me hate her more. Why should she get to be beautiful and smart? The gene police should make that illegal.

"Do you still keep a change of clothes in your duffel bag? Lyon over here could use them."

"Sure," she answers easily.

As if I could fit into stick-Barbie's clothes. Wait … how does Bennett know she carries a change of clothes?

I turn around, my embarrassment overrun by burning curiosity. My eyes flit between the two of them. There's a shit-ton of eye contact going on. One might even say longing stares. I push aside the evil part of me that wants to chain Bennett up in my basement so he can't be happy with anyone else. (Forget the fact that I don't have a basement.)

I'm about to gracefully protest and just grab some lighter fluid to set my hair on fire—it will sanitize, and it sounds way more appealing than trying to force my thighs into Zoe's clothes—when Seena surprises me. He steps over the body in the hall, comes my way, and shoves a duffel into my hands. "Always be prepared, Loser."

"Sir, yes, sir," I hug the bag to myself. "You are the best second-best-friend ever." Thank goodness! "OMG. I owe you apples. And carrots. And sugar cubes."

Seena rolls his eyes but grins.

"I'm gonna use the bathroom to change. In case the locks are broken in there, this is everyone's warning," I say as I head away.

"Don't touch anything," Flowers calls out.

I don't bother to respond. Instead, I swing my chicken leg around awkwardly and limp toward the bathroom.

"Fox, you're molting," Flowers shouts after me.

I flip him the bird. Like I can help shedding feathers. It's not a conscious decision. My stupid power makes my leg go chicken. At least molting means my leg is turning human again. I shoo a couple chickie pups, who are rapidly growing bigger as they trail after me—yips turning to barks and chick fuzz turning to feathers—out the door as I take refuge in the bathroom.

I peel off my nasty puked-on uniform and start the faucet. I expect the water to appear brown in this broken-down house, but thankfully it's clear. I rinse my hair, careful not to let it touch the sink, which is ringed in more grime than a gravedigger's shower drain. It's so gross there are raised green stripes on the sides, like some kind of fuzzy fungus.

"Gross and super gross." I totally take a photo of the dirty sink with my phone and send it to JR.

Where are you? she texts.

Luke's place.

Break up. Now. Not even joking.

I'm kidding.

Not funny.

I grab Seena's clothes out of his bag and stuff them between my knees. Then I pick my dirty uniform off the tile floor and go to put it in Seena's duffel only to find out it's got a thin layer of short blue hairs on it.

OMG! Those better not be supernatural pubes.

I hold my uniform by two fingers and lower it carefully into Seena's duffel. I'm seriously debating if it should go straight to the dumpster. But I don't get paid until next week and I've only got three uniforms—dagnabbit. Maybe my neighbor, Mrs. Snow, will take pity on me and help me out so I can get the thing dry cleaned.

I check my underwear. At least nothing got on it. I'm wearing a cute little navy-blue lace set because I was hoping I'd get to meet up with Luke later.

I've just pulled the t-shirt and gym shorts from between my knees when the bathroom door bursts open.

"Ahh!" I screech, holding Seena's clothes up like a shield.

"Whoa!" Flowers holds a hand over his eyes.

"What the heck, you granny panty!" I screech, "Have you lost your effing—"

Flowers hand clamps over my mouth and shoves me against the wall, pressing into me. "Don't!" he growls.

I get quiet.

He lets go of me and my feet slide back down to the floor.

His eyes flicker over my lacy lingerie before he deliberately stares around at the floor.

"Are you going to explain?" I huff.

"Put a shirt on."

I toss on Seena's white shirt only to find the front has a lovely little saying on it. "You fartled me." I roll my eyes. Nerd humor. I pull on the blue gym shorts, tighten the string at the waist, and toss my feet back into my shoes, grateful for the socks that protected me from the nasty floor.

"A lizard-bear was running away. I thought he got under the door," Flowers mumbles, eyes still down.

"Yeah, right. Did someone dare you to come in here?" I narrow my eyes.

Flowers glares at me for that. "Like I'd ever wanna see you naked by choice, -ox," his eyes widen.

"-ox, -ox … what the -uck?!" Flower's voice takes on a tone I don't think I've ever heard before. Panic.

"What's wrong?" I ask.

"-ucking hell!" Flowers stares at me.

My eyes widen and my stomach drops.

Oh shit. I said 'lost.' That's my magic trigger word.

I try and keep my face blank. He's gonna kill me. I said Flowers lost his *effing* ... Fudge berries! My hand flies to my mouth. Flowers said -uck, -ox. Shizzle sticks. I don't think he can say the letter 'f' anymore.

Diego Flores' fist smashes the bathroom wall. "What the hell? What did you do to me, -ox ... Lyon?"

I cringe backwards and bite my lip. "Ummm ..."

"You -ix it. -ix it now!"

"How do you know I did this?" I go for a flimsy cop out.

"You said lost! You said it! Now I can't -ucking talk!"

I did. But I didn't mean to. "You scared me!" (I don't say— "Sorry, but hey, guess what? At least I didn't finish the sentence. Because I was gonna ask if you'd lost your effing mind." Why don't I say that? Because Flowers looks like he wants to add to the body count this place has going.)

I back up to the shower curtain. It's got white soap scum all over it. But if it comes to choosing scum or angry Flowers, I'm going with scum. A cool breeze hits me. I realize the window in this room is open. Probably because it's so old the fan doesn't work. I turn my head toward it, debating whether I could escape, but the window is high and pretty small, about the size of a loaf of bread. No way my ass is squeezing out of that thing.

"Undo it," Flowers growls.

"I dunno how," I whimper, trying to make myself as small as possible.

He looms over me. "You're gonna learn."

I nod, trying to scrunch even more. His hatred pours over me like lava. I'm pretty sure my bones are melting.

Bennett's head pokes around the door. "Everything okay in here?"

Flowers backs off a step and I come out of the standing semi-fetal position I was in. I breathe a sigh of relief.

"No," Flowers growls.

"What's wrong?" Bennett's concern is a lifeline. I want to jump in his arms and hide my face in his neck and tell him to flame the mean kitty cat. Only, I can't. Because even if it was an accident, I've seriously fucked up.

I bite my lip and nervously make eye contact with my commanding officer. That's a big mistake. We've got a weird history. We dated seriously a couple years ago, recently hooked up, and then broke up about a month ago, and his feelings still simmer in his gaze. He wants to get back together. I just want to survive working together. I break away from his stare.

"Um ... I think I kinda ... sorta ... maybe ... made Flowers lose his ability to say f-words."

"You gave him a cursing curse?" Bennett sounds disappointed in me. "Ly, I know how much you hate that thing. Why would you ever curse someone—"

"No, no!" I wave my arms, accidentally whacking Flowers. I immediately pull back, lest I lose an arm. "I mean, he can't say the letter F."

"As in—"

Flowers interjects. "As in the letter between E and G. She - uckin' screwed me over, Boss."

"He burst in here while I was naked!"

Flames jump in Bennett's eyes as he swivels to glare at Flowers. "What?"

"I was chasing a damn lizard bear! You're missing the point!"

"You're missing the point! She could sue you for sexual harassment!"

Flowers and I both freeze.

"Um … it was an accident," I whisper. No way in hell do I want Flowers to get even more mad at me. And it *was* an accident. We both had an accident. I'm not suing him. He's not killing me. Even steven. Right?

Flowers' eyes don't seem to say even steven. They seem to say, "You'd better stick a mirror around every corner before you turn it. Because I'll be waiting."

I close my eyes and wish I had a fairy godmother who could wave her wand and make this all go away. Too bad fairy godmothers are just made up.

"Permission to be released -rom this assignment," Flowers requests, growling when he can't say 'from' properly.

My eyes pop open and stare at Bennett who eyes the two of us. A vein pulses in Bennett's neck. Not a good sign. "Denied. You two are always at each other's throats. You need to learn to work together like grown-ups."

I meet Flowers eyes before he stomps out of the bathroom.

Yeah. Fat chance. (Or … as Flowers now says, "-at chance.")

4

I walk out of the bathroom to hear Zoe Nightingale talking with Bennett in the front hall.

Jane Doe's body has been put into a body bag for transport and a couple wizards are levitating it toward the front door.

"Definitely homicide. I'll have to test down at the lab, but it's looking like a hex right now," Zoe sing-song says as she pulls off her medical examiner gloves, "If she was the dealer, which is what it looks like, this coulda' been anyone. Boss, addict, competition … a lotta people could have wanted her dead."

Well, baby shit. It looks like our assignment to bust up a nap shack just got upgraded to a homicide investigation. I glance around to share a look with Seena but he's nowhere to be found.

Zoe leans into Bennett and I take a step toward them—what? I'm allowed to ask the Commander for my assignment. If it just so happens to interrupt his conversation with a hot ME, that's totally a coincidence.

Flowers pops up out of nowhere, intercepting me with a gleam in his eyes. I know that gleam. Nothing good ever comes of that gleam, and right now it's got a murderous glint added to it. Not because this is a homicide investigation either. Nope, that glint is all for me. FML.

"Lyon … good news, you get to practice evidence collection."

My stomach sinks as any hope of an early morning flies out the window. "Yippee. Where's the team?"

"Oh no. No team. You need to learn *every* aspect of collection. So … I think you can do this one yoursel- … alone." The loss of the letter 'f' turns his last word into a deadly growl that makes my toes curl.

An entire house? By myself? With a staircase that's been busted by a rampaging hippo and animal shit every two feet?

A cop comes running toward Flowers and me, gagging. He shoves past the wizards on the stoop and bends over to retch into the grass. His partner follows behind leisurely. It's the first time I've ever envied a zombie. His dead nose is unaffected by the nastiness around us.

Flowers looks up from dealing with me to ask the zombie, "Tony, what happened to him?"

Tony jerks his head behind him and a little piece of loose flesh flaps on his neck. "Hall closet stuffed with jars of urine. Some of it was pretty rank, I guess. I'll call out the HAZMAT team." Tony ambles off and I stare after him for a second. (He's the only zombie on the force. Apparently, the first brain he tried to eat belonged to a witch doctor, who gave him back some of his mental faculties.)

Flowers nods at Tony's retreating back.

This urine-closet discovery does not bode well for me. I secretly wish speed upon the HAZMAT team so that I don't end up repeating puke-cop's performance.

I eye the dark hallways and count at least four more doors. Dammit. The likelihood of at least one of those being infested with something foul is pretty damn high.

It's official. Flowers wants me dead.

All over a stupid letter.

I close my eyes and remind myself that I'm actually good at this job. That normally, I like this job. That the feeling I get when I solve a case is worth it. I go home proud of myself and walk on air the following day. I don't want to give all of that up just because I accidentally ticked off some tiger by erasing a letter from his vocab. I mean, really, who uses 'f' anyway? It's not that important. If it was a pivotal letter, if it

45

was super-popular, it'd be in the finale on that show *Fortune's Wheel*. Fuck. I just used 'f' in my thoughts like five times.

I bow my head in defeat. I'm gonna have to let Flowers punish me. (There it is again! Flowers! Crap. Diego Flores can't even say his own name now. I picture him trying to renew his license at the DMV—department of magical variations, where all magical beings have to register when they become adults—those crones that work there would pass their shared eyeball around and give him a hell of a time.) "Lead on, sir," I capitulate.

Flowers narrows his eyes, expecting a punchline, but when I just stand there awaiting orders, he jerks his head and has me follow him to the dilapidated home office across from the living room, where a half dozen paunchy, thirty-something guys in handcuffs stand around ... in the buff.

"Whoa!" I shield my eyes.

"Gotta truck coming for them, don't worry about them," Flowers bends to pick up an evidence collection toolbox.

For a second, I regret Flower's attitude. Because, hey, the dude's got a seriously nice ass. But the attitude that comes with it is all hole.

"Excuse me," one of the naked guys says to me. "Are you the part-chicken shifter?"

"Uh ..." I look at Flowers in askance.

"Your leg," he rolls his eyes as he hefts the toolbox.

"Oh. Um …" I don't really know how to answer that question. Technically, I'm part fae. My mother is pure fairy, with a strange mix of all kinds of fae in our family tree. My dad was human. So, I was born a fairy without wings and without a lotta power. The only supernatural things about me until this fall were the blue jewel embedded in my chin and my quick-healing powers. Or so I thought.

Recently … things have gotten a little weird. I can lose things, like rampaging hippos or letters. And there's the little matter of my blood that I've been avoiding. I have three messages from the doctor at the hospital about my missed appointment. I was supposed to go in to double-check my blood and magic test. A test that came back stating I was part demon.

I think they mixed up my blood sample. That's gotta be it. No way my mother would associate with a demon. She's too snooty for that.

I briefly wonder if that doctor's test was wrong. Flowers didn't think I was part chicken before … but I guess it's still a possibility. I mean, if I was only part chicken, maybe I wouldn't set off his tiger-shifter instincts.

I turn to the naked speaker who asked about my leg. I keep my gaze high—no need to add the sight of shriveled gobblers to the freak show this house has turned into—and ask, "Why do you want to know?"

47

Naked guy clears his throat. "I'm Lamar. you know, I just wanted to see if you might wanna get coffee sometime. Talk chicken-shifting."

Some nude dude wants to grab coffee with a part-chicken cop? Why? It dawns on me. The Nappies wore off. The shifters grew up. Flowers probably force-fed them 'human' potion to make them shift. (Humans are easier to arrest than animals. Plus, after the whole Darrell-cat incident last week, Bennett gave us a lecture on protocol that I'm certain Flowers thinks is gospel.) I take a second to stare at naked guy and his friends. One guy bobbles his head back and forth on his neck. He kinda looks like a bird. *Oh my ghosts in the graveyard!* These are the chickie pups. And I just got asked out by one.

I burst into laughter.

"Man, naked and arrested is not the time. Not the time."

He huffs indignantly.

I ignore his offended naked ass and follow Flowers to the kitchen, swiping at the tears that come to my eyes. "Darn, that was funny."

Flowers doesn't grin. I realize I just said another word that he can't say anymore. Funny.

I shut my trap. Flowers just points to the kit and has me take out a spell detector. It's a little blue scanner, kinda like ultraviolet. But instead of showing up white, spelled items or spell remnants pulse red. The more red things glow, the more magic was used on them. I toss on the green glasses that go with the scanner and start at the door frame.

Flowers stomps off to the living room to help Bennett and the others deal with the house occupants, pumping the Nappies out of their system with one spell, then turning them human with a potion. I get a decent view of it all from the kitchen as I scan the walls and countertops.

Grasshorse, the tiny grasshopper horse from the cage on the table, turns into a huge black guy with a green mohawk. He's naked, too. This time, though, I'm not protesting the nudity. Grasshorse is ripped. (Which I hardly notice, BTW. I am a professional.)

Flowers slaps cuffs on him and carefully recites, "You're under arrest … using an illegal substance." (I notice he just skips over the word 'for' completely.) "And you need to answer questions in connection with a homicide."

"What?" Grasshorse bursts out. "This was my first time here, dude! I didn't do anything! I didn't kill nobody."

Flowers doesn't answer, just has another lackey on the force haul the guy to the huge police van purring outside.

Grasshorse is upset the whole way, trying to convince the other officer he's innocent. "I just needed to relax, man! My girl's been stressing me out. Dammit, I need a damn cigarette," His voice fades as they get farther away. I watch through the front window as Grasshorse takes a seat on the van bench next to a naked chickie pup.

"We're gonna need to bleach our van," I mutter, thinking about all the naked asses that are touching it tonight.

"How nice that you volunteered," Flowers says.

"You're a camel toe," I grumble under my breath.

"What was that?"

I turn and scan the countertop, trying to act like I don't hear Flowers.

It doesn't work. He comes up behind me. "Want to repeat that, Lyon?" he growls.

"Not particularly," I mumble.

Flowers opens his mouth to cuss me out. At the same time, a furry creature skitters across the kitchen counter. Flowers lunges and grabs it. It looks like a furry black lizard, only the head's all wrong. It's—I lean forward to get a better look— got a bear head. A fuzzy lizard with a bear head. A lizard-bear.

Flowers holds the lizard-bear up triumphantly. "Haha. Got you, you sorry -ucker." Flower's lips thin and I can see a vein in his neck throb.

"I like to substitute in the word duck, personally," I offer helpfully.

That just makes Flowers give me the look of death again. Which would normally be way more intimidating, but suddenly the lizard-bear's tail falls off. It wriggles on the ground like a furry caterpillar.

Both Flowers and I curl our lips.

"Gross." I swear, as cases go, this is turning into the weirdest one yet.

Flowers marches out of the room with the lizard bear, leaving the wriggling tail for me to deal with. I step carefully around it and I get back to scanning.

My light hits the cutting board. The red pulse from the milk carton is bright but the red starburst from the knife on the board is nearly blinding.

"Crepes!" I shield my eyes.

Bennett runs into the room. "Ly, are you okay?"

I nod and point at the veggie knife. Some symbols are glowing on the side of it. Not just runes. But a complicated-looking magical equation full of numbers and symbols. "Commander, I think I found the murder weapon."

Bennett shields his eyes and looks at the knife. "Definitely looks hexed. Nice work."

I pull an evidence baggy out the toolbox Flowers carried in here and I bag the knife. I'm about to write on the baggie when someone nearly bowls me over from behind. I go sprawling next to the toolbox. My face slams into the linoleum and I get an up close view of the hairy lizard tail. Super gross. There are like red tubes plopping out of the middle where the tail used to be attached. You know those toddler duplo building blocks? It's like an ooey goey version of those sticking out of the black furry tail. I have to tamp down on my gag reflex.

"Sorry, Loser," Seena hauls himself off me and offers me a hand so I can stand up. That's when I notice that I fell right onto the hexed knife. Thank goodness I was holding it flat. Otherwise … I shiver.

"What the funion?" I ask Seena. Why the hell is he shoving into me?

He straightens his glasses and points at the ceiling, where a panel hangs down on two hinges. "Secret passageway. Dumps out here."

All is totally forgiven. My near death. The lizard-tail trauma. I had a serious mystery addiction in my pre-teen years. And secret passageways are like the holy grail of mysteries. I stare up at the ceiling in awe. I've never seen a real-life secret passageway before. "Show me!"

Seena clears his throat. "Umm … actually, I need to speak with Commander French."

"What? Why?"

"Because I found a second body. And it's a dragon."

5

I follow Seena but stay a few feet back as he tells Bennett what he found.

The blood drains from Bennett's face and Zoe touches his arm.

Dragons are hard to kill.

If a dragon's dead here, it won't be an accident.

And if a dragon's dead, Bennett's gonna flip.

I watch my ex take a deep breath. His green eyes flash with red-hot flames for a second. But he controls himself and doesn't shift in public. He breathes deeply through his nose a few times and then nods at Seena, wordlessly telling my friend to lead the way. Seena leads Bennett down the side hall, past the HAZMAT team.

Zoe follows. So do I.

We file past the guys in suits carrying out jars of yellow and clear liquid. A foul smell wafts from a cracked jar. Damn. It smells like cat piss! I bury my nose in my elbow. I don't wanna get sick. I hold my breath until my eyes water and then gulp air. Luckily, the rancid pee smell is gone at that point and I can focus on the matter at hand: dragons.

Seena goes carefully up the half-smashed stairs and into a bedroom that's full of human baby cribs crowded so close that the sides touch. Luckily, the room is empty.

Seena walks right into the closet and presses on the wall. A panel opens. He flicks on his flashlight and shines it into the secret passageway. Unlike the secret passageways from my imagination, this one is not coated in dust and cobwebs. It might be cleaner than the actual house. (Which is a low bar, sure, but still.) Open-topped wooden crates full of straw line either side of the aisle. I can see different illegal potions peeking through the crates. Seena ducks his head, because the passageway isn't full height, and walks in.

The rest of us follow.

My heart thrums in my chest. I hope Seena's wrong. For Bennett's sake, for the dragon's sake … for all our sakes, I hope he's wrong. Dragon vengeance is brutal. If there is a dead dragon, his clan's retaliation won't end until everyone associated with the murder has been flamed.

I duck into the dark passage and switch on my own flashlight, shining it so Zoe and I can watch where we step. We shuffle forward.

The air inside the cramped secret hallway is stale. And there's a sickly-sweet smell that I hope is not what I think it is.

The passageway widens and Seena leads us all around the corner. There's a small alcove, just above the kitchen. On the far side of the alcove, the floor gapes open with the trap door that leads to the kitchen. Light streams up through it.

Against the wall of the alcove, curled up in a ball, as if he were just sleeping, is a tiny baby dragon. But unlike a live dragon, which is full of iridescent color, this dragon is grey. The sickly-sweet smell is coming from him. Seena was right. The dragon's dead.

Crap. I look at Bennett; his shoulders are tight. His right hand shakes.

I push past Zoe and latch onto Bennett's hand. His breathing is heavy, and he squeezes my hand as if he's trying to crush it.

I make eye contact with him and just hold it. There's nothing I can say.

His dragon instincts are going haywire. I can see his scales flicker like shadows underneath his skin. I just try to hold eye contact and breathe deep through my mouth as he fights to get a handle on himself.

Zoe rubs her hand down Bennett's arm, giving me a look, but I ignore her. This isn't personal right now. Bennett's freaking. His dragon instincts are raging. He needs a focal point, so he doesn't full-on shift at a crime scene. I start counting out loud as I inhale and exhale and he matches his breath to mine.

When Zoe sees I've got Bennett calming down, she goes over to examine the dragon. She snaps on some gloves, which causes Bennett's skin to heat up and me to have to start the whole calming process all over again. (Dammit woman, don't you know anything about hot-headed dragons?)

Seena just runs his flashlight awkwardly over the space. "Hmm," he crouches and pulls an evidence baggy out of his pocket.

"What is it?" Bennett rasps, smoke curling out of his lips as if he's smoking a cigar. But he's not. He's simply smoking.

"Pack of matches," Seena shrugs. "Might not be anything, but maybe we can lift a print..."

Bennett nods and breathes out, releasing a long stream of smoke right into my face.

I can't help it. I start coughing.

"Sorry," he releases my hands and pats my back awkwardly.

I smack my chest and turn away from the smoke, my eyes watering a bit. "No problem. You good?"

"Yup. Thanks." He clenches his fists but I don't see scales wavering under his skin anymore, so I think he's telling the truth.

"Anytime," I cough once more and then turn to Zoe. Technically, she outranks me since I'm still at the Academy. But I ask anyway, since I'm not sure Bennett can talk just yet, "What does it look like?"

She narrows her eyes at me but turns to Bennett and says, "I'm not seeing any hex like the old woman's finger. Given the fact that he's baby-sized and his pupils are blown out … I'm guessing he mighta' overdosed on Nappies."

Seena crouches and stares around at the ground. Then he snaps on some plastic gloves and swipes a finger over the dragon's body. "It's hard to tell with all our footprints, but he's got some dust on him. Looks like he might have died elsewhere and been stashed here. Maybe in one of those cages. Like they gave him too much."

A low growl rumbles in Bennett's chest. "You mean they realized he was dead and didn't wanna deal with him."

Crap! That growl's a warning. He's on the edge. I grab Seena's hand and push Zoe back the way we came.

"Any fire resistance spells?" I whisper to Zoe. "Those would be good right about now."

"Remember," I tell Bennett, even as I get everyone to back away, "if you shift, you'll destroy evidence and we won't be able to find the killer."

Bennett's hands clench. His whole body starts to shake as he tries to reign the dragon part of himself in.

Zoe whispers in my ear. "I've got a calming spell. Should I try it on him?"

I nod. "Yup." Idiot woman. I take back all the smart-jealousy I've had. Why the hell didn't Zoe mention a calm spell earlier when I was doing the whole zen breath thing? Did she think that was just for funsies?

Zoe whips out a wand and draws some silvery lines in the air.

I warn Bennett so he doesn't freak any further, "Calming spell coming your way."

The silver lines float over to him. I don't see them do anything really, but Bennett stops shaking. Gradually, he stops smoking.

He takes one last look at the body and grabs the radio on his shoulder. "Flores, get up to the second floor. I'm off this investigation. You're it."

Bennett doesn't wait for a response; he just shoves his way past us out of the secret passageway. I can hear him stomp down the stairs.

Seena and I make eye contact.

"I'm pretty sure secret passages have been ruined for me forever," I say.

Seena just shakes his head, glasses gleaming from my flashlight. "I'm pretty sure babies have been ruined for me forever."

Good point.

6

E vidence collection is a bitch. Or I'm evidence
collection's bitch.

My back hurts, my hands hurt, and I feel like
bathing in a tub of bleach after going through that house. I'm
not a clean freak by any means, but even the vents in that
place were covered in grime. It was literally blowing dirty air
all over that house.

I shower at home, trying very hard not to look at my hands
or my skin. My fingers hurt from using the tweezers so
much. I vaguely wonder if I can file a worker's comp claim
for finger strain. There were at least a billion hair samples.
Apparently, Flowers was right about shifters loving Nappies.
So, so many hairs. And even though I scanned the murder

weapon almost right away, Flowers made me magically scan every other utensil in that kitchen.

He did relent on other evidence collection, though. With two bodies and the size of the house, it would have taken me weeks to do it alone. A couple wizards came in and put my by-hand techniques to shame. They had that place scanned in a couple hours.

I wish I was a frickin' wizard.

"Flowers is a stinkin' glitter bomb," I mutter as I soap up, annoyance eating at me.

I have to pause during my hair washing three times. Yes, my fingers hurt that bad. No, I'm not just being dramatic.

When I finally finish with my shower, I blow dry my hair and check my texts.

I had texted Bennett just to check on him but he hasn't responded.

I had also texted Luke. And he did answer.

Hell yes I want to see you. How is not seeing you even an option?

He still wants to meet me at Wendel's. My heart soars. I fist pump, I'm that excited. It's almost dawn, but he says he's got a spell to protect him from daylight for a few hours. I smile and savor that sweet giddiness of new relationships for a second as I picture his dimples.

Then I pop an ibuprofen and slide into a cute sweater dress with chunky boots. I toss on a red jacket. My mother hates me in red. Says blondes shouldn't wear red. So, obviously, I love it.

I'm waiting on the corner for my Broomer when I see Tabby Blue and Sarah Snow strolling up the street.

I wave. "What are you ladies doing out at the crack of dawn?" I ask.

The pair slows down when they reach me. Sarah Snow's my seventy-something southern sweetheart of a neighbor. She lives downstairs. Her BFF, Tabby Blue, is a pistol, a naughty old lady with bottle-thick glasses who's rich as can be but doesn't give two shits about little things like legality. She's everything I wanna be one day.

"Well, don't you look dolled up, sugar," Sarah smiles, "I like that dress."

I do a silly little spin. "Got a date with Luke."

Both women tilt their heads. "Aww, now isn't that the sweetest. I knew he was a keeper. That's why I kept nudging you two together," Sarah says.

I look at her oddly. It was over a month before we got together. And I don't remember much nudging.

Tabby rolls her eyes. "I still like the dragon, but I have to agree, your matchmaking sense was right on with this one."

"Matchmaking?" I ask. Sarah's making it sound like she did something here.

"Yeah, I kept him warm for you. Chatting him up. Little tidbits here and there … teasers. Gotta tease men, get in their heads." She winks, "I'm an expert."

"You've got Clarence down at the bingo hall wrapped around your finger, that's for sure," Tabby nods.

"How come you're meeting Luke so late?" Sarah glances at the sky, which is already getting light.

I sigh. "Kinda ticked off Flowers again." I tell them about my night and how I accidentally used the 'lost' word.

Sarah's hand flies to her heart. "Well, surely, he knew it was an accident. You're too galdarn sweet to have done something like that on purpose!"

"Yeah, don't think he sees it that way. He tried to make me do all the evidence collection for an entire house myself."

"That shit!" Tabby pushes her glasses up her nose. "I should go kick him in the shins for you."

I smile, picturing it. "That's alright, Tabby. But thanks for the offer. Maybe I'll take you up on it after I clean the butt cheek prints off the police van."

"What?!" I enjoy their outrage as I tell them about how Flowers has arranged for tomorrow night's torture as well.

After the cursing has settled down, Tabby asks, "You didn't get photos of all those naked shifters, did you?" she goes for casual, but I can hear the hopeful edge in her tone.

"Nope. I wasn't on photo duty."

She *tsks*.

Sarah sighs, tapping her chin. "You know, this Diego Flores always seems to have it out for you, honey."

I roll my eyes as I spot my Broomer in the distance. "That's because he thinks I don't take work seriously enough. But you can't take every second seriously."

Tabby shakes her head. "I had a husband like that. Number four. All he thought about was work, work, work."

Sarah cocks her head. "Well, now, I know you wouldn't stand for that. How'd you get him to snap out of it?"

"How do ya' think?" Tabby raises her brows.

I try very hard not to think about how she got hubby four to snap out of it. There are some mental images I don't need.

"Oh! Well, that's it!" Sarah smiles and claps her hands. "We can fix this!"

I raise up a hand, a little bit of worry sparking inside my chest. "Fix what?" I don't think I want them fixing anything to do with Flowers.

"Well, isn't it obvious? Flowers needs to focus on something other than work."

"You mean he needs to get laid," Tabby interjects.

Sarah waves her hand. "More than that. He needs a girlfriend. He needs love. We can use my matchmaking abilities, I mean, they worked so well with Ly and Luke ... we just have to find the perfect woman for him." She smiles and I can almost see cartoon hearts blooming in her eyes.

My stomach drops. This is a bad idea. A terrible idea. I wait for Tabby to say so.

"I have a couple friends with single granddaughters..."

No. I get chills. Tabby's response is all wrong. I start shaking my head. The absolute last thing I need, in the entire universe, is for them to interfere with my work life. With Flowers' life. He knows they're my friends. He'll think I put them up to this. He's already at threat-level red. I seriously think he might nuke me if they try this.

"No. Flowers doesn't need a matchmaker."

Sarah looks at me skeptically. "He's dating someone?"

"Yes!" I grasp at her excuse desperately. "Totally dating someone."

"Who?" Sarah folds her hands over her chest skeptically.

"I... um—he doesn't talk about personal stuff at work!" There! That should work, right? Truth. He doesn't share anything.

"Then how do you know?" Sarah asks.

"She's lying," Tabby sounds bored and dismissive as she turns to Sarah. "I think I know the perfect woman. She's tall, but not too tall, and her grandma says she likes rock-climbing. Mountain-climbing. All that. Which is something an athletic man like him would like."

"I'm not lying!" I screech, as my Broomer swoops down to hover near us.

"Lyon Fox?" The witch on the broom looks between the three of us.

"Yeah, just a sec."

"You're charged for wait time," she says.

I ignore her. There are more pressing things right now. Things like preventing this disaster. I can practically see the excitement building between Sarah and Tabby as they face each other. This is a brand new, shiny project. They aren't gonna let go easily. They want to play matchmaker? Fine. We just need them to direct their energy at someone other than my very angry boss.

"Look, you two should totally try the matchmaking thing," I try a soothing tone. "You'd be great at it. But you should start a company. You should charge for it. Your services are worth something. You shouldn't go wasting your talents for free on my boss."

Tabby's eyes widen behind her glasses. The magnification is so big that she looks like an owl. "Now, there's an idea."

Sarah taps a finger against her cherry red lips. "I like it. We could call it … Snow Blue … kinda like Snow White. Our slogan could be: Get your happily ever after here."

"Blue Snow is alphabetical, and funny," Tabby points out.

They turn toward one another, nit-picking and arguing over names.

I let out a deep breath. Thank goodness. Crisis averted.

I walk over to the witch and sling my leg onto the broom behind her. "Wendel's please."

We rise into the air and my thoughts turn toward Luke. But as we start to pick up speed, Tabby's yell sounds in my ears.

"Don't worry, Lyon! We'll still fix up Flowers for free!"

FML.

I BEMOAN MY LIFE TO LUKE, AND HE LISTENS PATIENTLY, watching, and smelling as I devour a giant, warm-from-the-oven brownie at Wendel's.

"We'll find a way to run interference with Tabby and Sarah," he reassures me, rubbing my back. "They won't get you fired. I promise."

I sigh and lean into him, letting my food coma and his company bliss me out for a minute. Then I turn to him and ask, "How was your night?" We've seen each other pretty much every other night since we officially started dating.

He sighs and runs a hand through his shoulder-length blond hair. I love his hair. "Annoyed clients. Had a shipment run late. If they'd paid the extra for teleportation, it wouldn't have been a problem. But they paid for standard shipping so —" Luke runs a caster business. Not a spell-caster business. Oh no, he builds custom wheels and ships them off to people.

"I'm sorry. People are dumb," I hate dumb people. Especially those who can erase the dimples from Luke's face. He should always be smiling. His smile is captivating.

"That they are," he agrees.

"Anything else?"

"Had dinner with my mom last morning."

"How's she?"

He sighs again. "Had to hand down a position to a daughter after the mom passed away. So, she's kinda down."

"Wait, what? Here?" I didn't hear about any deaths other than the case Seena and I had stumbled into—did someone else get killed?

"Overseas. Positions with my mother are ... handed down through the generations."

"Oh. Is that normal?" Luke's mom, or sire as vamps call them, is none other than Cookie Gonzalez, notorious leader of the Crypts gang. Luke's straight as an arrow. But his mom is *not*.

Luke nods. "Pretty standard in her line of work." Thankfully, he changes the subject quickly, "She asked me about you."

I tense. "Oh?"

Luke's hand runs down my arm, soothing me. I love that he loves to touch me. This is only our fourth date as a couple, and every single time, he's found an excuse to run his fingers through my hair or put his arm around my shoulders. He uses that touch now, interlacing our fingers as I watch. It used to make me nervous. But, now, it just makes me feel adored. "Hey, Mom just generally asked about you, it wasn't anything bad. She seemed ... excited. Maybe even overly excited, to be honest."

"I just worry, you know, about the cop thing."

Luke's hand reaches my chin and he turns me to look at him. "Hey, don't worry about that. If anyone needs to worry, it should be her."

My eyes flicker between his, uncertain. "Things might get weird for you. At some point. That's not a deal breaker?"

"Oh, we're onto this discussion already? Deal breakers?" he raises his brows.

I swallow hard, my heart thumping. Shit. Why'd I say that? Damn. Now it's awkward. I definitely do not want to discuss deal breakers right now. I have yet to share with Luke the tiny, insignificant fact that my blood could turn him human. I'm so not ready for that conversation. Luckily, biting is basically a declaration of love in the vamp community. So, I have time. So long as my stupid mouth doesn't shoot off and ruin things for me. "Sorry. Too deep, too early. I have a problem with doing that." I lean back in the booth, trying to move away without being obvious.

Luke's not having it. He grabs my legs and pulls them on top of his own, so that I'm sideways in the booth, knees draped over his thighs.

"Hey, I'm fine with any conversation you want to have," he smiles. "I'm not scared."

"Well, I am," I grab my milk, eager to have something to do. I suck at the straw until it's slurping drops out of the bottom of the cup.

73

Luke just watches, his lips pressed together in a patient smile. "Are you done?"

I nod.

My phone buzzes in my pocket, giving me a much-needed excuse to look away from his enchanting blue eyes. "Sorry." I pull it out. It's another text from that annoying doctor at the hospital. "Ugh. I hate doctors."

"Doctors? Are you okay? Do you need to text back?" he touches my arm, concerned.

"Nah," I wave it off. "It's just some test they want me to retake. They made a mistake and think I'm part demon. Ha! How dumb is that? How about we pretend I didn't make things awkward and just snuggle?" I lean on him. His pecs are amazing. And the cologne he's wearing is a perfect winter sky and pine mixture.

"Do you maybe want to snuggle … at my place?" he asks.

I sit up straight. We haven't done that yet. We haven't done 'it' yet. We've known each other awhile but have only technically gone on a couple dates. My mouth dries out.

"We don't have to—" Luke says.

"Hell yes," I breathe. And then I kiss him, hard.

His eyes are burning when I let him go. "Well, then, you might need to get your legs off me, so I can get out of this booth."

"This is a test," I arch a brow at him. "A test of your strength and flexibility. I need to know what I'm working with."

He tries so hard not to let the laughs take over his chest as he plays along, scooping me further into his lap. "I'm gonna ace this test."

"I dunno," I trail my arms over his ripped biceps. "I grade hard."

He slides us around out of the booth and then hitches my legs around his waist so I'm in front of him. "Well, I work hard."

I lean forward and whisper in his ear. "Good. One rule: no biting."

He groans but nods.

He holds onto me with one hand and pulls something out of his pocket with the other. We're out the door and—*blink*—we're at Luke's place in half a second. I'm still in his arms.

"Whoa, teleportation. Pulling out the big guns." He's not a wizard. That spell must have cost him a pretty penny. I raise my eyebrows. "I'm impressed, Mr. Hawkins."

He winks as he grabs his key. "Only the best for my girl."

Is it weird that my knees turn to jelly at that? Hearing him call me his girl?

He invites me in (vampire habit) and when he switches on the lights, my jaw drops in shock.

"Marry me." The words are out of my mouth before the thought has even fully formed in my brain.

Luke laughs and comes up behind me. His arms encircle my waist. "You like?"

I nod, open-mouthed. Luke's front room is big. It's full of shelves, floor to ceiling. And every single shelf is filled with books.

Cremate me now. Because I've died and gone to book-lover's heaven.

I slide out of his hands, walk over to the nearest shelf, and run my fingers down the spine of a leather-bound book.

Luke comes up behind me and presses against my back. His arms wrap around me. "I wanna know you … in the bibliophile way. Spread those pages for me, baby."

I laugh so hard I snort. "That's so corny, hot, and ridiculous in the same moment."

He spins me around and shrugs before draping his hands over my shoulders. "I know. I thought it was the perfect pickup line for you."

I smile and my heart goes mushy. "It totally was."

He winks and whispers, "Read my lips." Then he mouths, "Bedroom."

I slink out from under his arms and say, "Just so you know … I only read books with 'happy endings.'" I use air quotes.

Luke grins. "Oh, I'll give you a happy ending."

Then he sweeps me off my feet and carries me away.

Damn. This guy might not be just a happy ending. A scary little voice in my head whispers he might be my happily ever after.

7

I wake up at Luke's in midafternoon. He's still out cold (yeah, I'm punny). But I am riding high from—you know. I can't fall back asleep and staring at hotness incarnate is only entertaining for about thirty minutes or so.

After I've memorized every one of Luke's freckles, I roll out of bed and get dressed. I search my phone for dry cleaners. As much as I wish I could buy some over-the-counter spell to get out the baby puke, I'd taken a look in Seena's bag before I'd met Luke. And the puke was glowing yellow. So, whatever had spit on me wasn't pure human. There's no telling what is in that puke and no way I'm hand washing that uniform and letting it touch my skin.

I find an all-day cleaner's close to my place.

I write Luke a note detailing every naughty thing I'll do to him later and walk back to my apartment. It's a long walk, but I'm pepped up and full of energy. I text JR even though I know she's asleep.

I slept over! Call me so we can grab drinks and I can gush.

I smile at a couple elves who are packing up their cleaning equipment outside an office building.

When I turn onto my street, all is quiet. Part of me wonders if Sarah Snow noticed that I didn't come home after my date. I dread and am excited to talk to her about it at the same time.

Inside my apartment, I get dressed for our evening workout, pack my clothes for the office portion of the night, then another set of junk clothes—because I'm pretty certain Flowers was serious about having me bleach the police van—and finally, I grab the duffel. Arms stuffed, I make my way down the street to Sue's Cleaners, a shop that has the classy slogan: *We Like It Dirty*. (I literally picked them for this slogan, because who could resist that?)

I thought I'd be the only person there, because really, who's out at 4:00 p.m.? But, nope. Wrong-o.

Two people stand in line in front of me. A wizard with a very sad droopy little hat taps his foot to a song in his head and whistles while he waits in line. In front of him, a frantic brownie with fourteen different vamp cloaks is arguing with the navy-haired girl behind the counter.

"I have a coupon for each one of these," the brownie squeaks. She looks like a miniature human, skinny with curly hair, properly proportioned—she just happens to be three feet tall instead of five.

The attendant, whose name tag reads *Marian,* sighs and rubs her nose ring as she says, "Look at the sign. One coupon per customer." She points a tattooed hand at prominent sign on the wall.

"These are all for different vamps," the brownie argues. "They're each a customer."

Marian's eyes roll toward the ceiling. "You're literally going to make me ring up each one separately?"

"Yes. I have to provide them each with a receipt."

"You do realize that I'm likely to pee on every one of these capes once you leave, right?"

The brownie's jaw drops.

"If you make me run all those transactions, I will make sure those capes smell in a way that no one can get out." The irises in Marian's eyes turn yellow and her pupils narrow and elongate. She's some kind of shifter. And clearly pissed.

Personally, I think she's overreacting about the separate transaction thing. But I don't have a job that makes me work at 4:00 p.m. with coupon-obsessed brownies. I might be a little crazy, too, if that was the case.

Once the brownie gets over her shock, she's completely unintimidated by Marian's attitude. She drops the capes dramatically to the floor and raises her brow, staring straight at Marian. Then the brownie hops straight up in the air like some TV ninja, lands on the counter, and grabs Marian by the collar.

She shoves her face into the twenty-something girl's face and growls, "If you dare do anything to my clients' capes other than clean them, I will clean *you* up. I will erase every damn tattoo you've paid for, slowly and painfully. I will close up every hole you've put in your skin. And I will make sure your hair can never hold another dye again. You'll be mouse-brown forever!"

Marian's eyes widen. She jerks her head back, clutching protectively at her blue hair. "Fine."

The brownie hops back down and scoops up the cloaks and the coupons. She dumps them all onto the counter. "I've put names in all the pockets along with a list of stains that need to be removed. Take extra care with the ectoplasm stains on the one cloak. The ghost slime was pretty thick. I'll be back to pick them up in three hours." I watch as the badass, middle-aged, mom-looking brownie walks past me toward the door.

"There's an extra charge for ghost ectoplasm," Marian calls out.

"There's a coupon in the pile for that!" the brownie yanks open the door, making the bell on top of it tinkle, before she stalks out.

I bite my lip and make eye contact with the wizard. We both widen our eyes at one another, silently saying, "Well that was dramatic."

Marian rolls her eyes, gathers up all the cloaks and pushes them to the side of the counter. She leans forward on an elbow and says, "Next."

The wizard steps up and places his drooping hat carefully on the counter. "I need a stiffening spell, please."

Marian's expression is deadpan. "Of course, you do."

"I'd like to wait for it," the wizard says softly.

"Of course, you would," Marian stares at the wizard long enough for a blush to creep up his cheeks.

It takes me a minute, because, hey it's early, but then I finally realize what's going on. She has to use a stiffie potion for the hat. Stiffie solutions make hats hard and upright. They're illegal to use on people because they cause all kinds of weird complications. But if I had to guess, Mr. Wizard is going to stuff that hat onto something other than his head and hope the spell remnants affect it. Double gross.

I clear my throat. I decide to help the poor girl out. Clearly, this job sucks a big one. (Not the wizard's big one because … he obviously lacks in that department.) "You need that hat for an official meeting or something? Because otherwise, sir, I'd suggest you wait the designated time. As a member of Tres Lunas Police Department, we've been advised to tell citizens about the safety hazards of such spells. The stiffie solution is known to cause a lot of tissue damage when handled improperly. A man died just last week from complications after abusing it." (True story. Flowers made me read it. I don't mention the guy was rubbing raw undiluted powder on himself for two years … because, hey, making a point here.)

The wizard's eyes widen as he glances back at me. "Oh. Oh, I hadn't realized."

"Yeah, sure you hadn't," Marian rolls her eyes.

The wizard hurries out of the store, calling, "I'll be back in an hour or two."

Marian just shoves the hat to the side with the capes and gestures for me to come forward.

"Hope that keeps him out of your hair," I say as I set my duffel on the counter.

Marian shakes her head. "He'll just wait around the corner until you leave and then come back in here. He's a reg. But thanks for trying. Whatcha' got?"

"Some kind of weird baby puke. Not sure what species." I unzip the bag and show her my uniform.

Her eyes widen as she eyes my uniform. "You're really a cop?"

I shrug. "In training. Actually, right now, our jobs aren't that different. I just clean up crime scenes instead of capes."

Marian snaps on a pair of gloves and pulls my uniform out of the bag. Her eyes get huge as she sees the glowing yellow baby puke and the blue hair from the bathroom all over it. Her face grows pale.

"Are you okay?" I asked. "If that's like some kind of puke you're allergic to, don't worry about it. I can take it somewhere else."

"Nope. No, you're good. Just the smell," she says tightly, swallowing hard.

"Oh, okay. Good. You think it's something you can get out?" I ask.

She nods once. "Might not be ready 'til late."

I wave my hand dismissively. "No worries. I've got work all night. I won't be able to get back here 'til morning probably."

She nods and holds her breath as she carries my uniform into the back room.

I sigh. Her reaction to the puke was pretty bad. Hopefully that doesn't mean it was gonna cost me an arm and a leg. Unlike the brownie, I didn't come armed with a ton of coupons.

One chore down, I make my way to the Academy early. I stuff my things into a locker and head to the main room to stretch. I have a feeling Flowers is still gonna be angry about last night and will try to make the evening's exercise routine more painful than usual.

I'm surprised to find the lights on in the main room when I get there. I'm even more surprised to see Bennett pummeling the crap out of a practice dummy in the corner.

I debate saying hi but decide that him turning around to see me awkwardly watching would give a stalkerish vibe. So, I suck it up and walk over.

"Hey," I say.

He gives a giant roundhouse kick to the dummy that would have broken a real man's neck. "Hey."

"I texted."

"I saw."

I wait but he just keeps beating the dummy. Okay, then. I do one of those awkward lip smack things, where you don't really know what to say. "I'm gonna go stretch out before Flowers gets here."

Bennett nods but doesn't respond beyond that.

I walk to the far side of the room and sit down on a mat. I stretch, watching Bennett out of the corner of my eye. I feel bad for him. I mean, when fae were being attacked, I'd been scared for my family. And I'm just a part fairy. I don't have the clan bonds that dragons do.

Supposedly, dragons and their "clans" and werewolves and their "packs" are connected on this deeper, more intense level.

I really hope that the dragon wasn't from Bennett's old clan. I have no idea if Bennett still feels the connection even though he's gone rogue. I really don't know a lot. I sigh.

Part of me wishes I liked research like Seena. This job involves a lot of different species and all their drama. And I am coming to realize just how little I know about the world around me.

But ... instead of becoming Seena, what if I just asked him?

I grab my phone and text him.

Would Bennett be able to feel the connection to the dragon that died even if B's rogue?

"No," a rough voice above me startles me.

I drop my phone and look up. Bennett's standing over me. I didn't even hear him come up.

"No, I can't tell if he's from my old clan," Bennett's voice is gruff. "I can't tell anything anymore."

"Oh," my voice is small. I'm not sure what to say.

"He OD'd. Zoe confirmed it," Bennett says, staring at the wall.

My chest aches for him. "I'm so sorry," I whisper.

"She turned him human and everything back at the morgue. I watched … in case. I didn't recognize him."

I feel a rush of relief that Bennett's not dealing with one of his former clan members. I bite my lip and nod. His jaw doesn't unclench though. So, he doesn't feel that relief. A dead dragon still hurts him. Former clan or not.

"Zoe put time of death three days ago."

My stomach drops. "Before the old woman."

His nod is brief. "Her prints were on him. Figure Seena was right. He kicked it and she didn't want to deal with him, so she stuffed him up there. Zoe's gonna run a couple more tests but … yeah."

I shake my head. There's nothing to say to that. That woman was a drug dealer and a despicable creature.

Three days. I don't say anything but I'm worried. The dragon's clan hasn't noticed he's gone? They haven't been searching for him? My mind skims over our evening briefings. I haven't heard anything about a missing dragon in our meetings. I would have remembered that.

"They still searching for an identity?" I ask tightly.

Bennett nods. "Lotta overseas clans. Lotta dragons travel for work. He must not have been expected home yet. Zoe thinks she'll have an ID by tomorrow."

"Anything I can do?"

He shakes his head. "Nope. Nothing any of us can do." He runs a hand through his hair. "To be honest, I'm glad I handed the case over to Flowers. It was the right call. If I was running this case, I wouldn't give a damn who killed that old woman. As far as I'm concerned, she deserved worse than she got."

With that, Bennett tromps off to the men's locker room.

And I'm left wondering whether or not I agree with him. When a bad person bites it … how hard should the police work to catch the killer?

8

F lowers has none of Bennett's qualms. He's
practically giddy over the amount of evidence
we've hauled in against the Bloods, the troll gang
he thinks was running the nap shack. Or maybe it's the fact
that he's in charge of this case. Or maybe he's just dipped
into all the drugs we've hauled into the evidence locker.
Seriously, he smiled like three times during our exercises
tonight. That never happens.

I ponder the possibilities as I label yet another bag of hair
samples. "1,472." I use a black sharpie to write the sample
number on an evidence bag. When half your drug addicts
shift to animal form for their nap time, there are a shit ton of
hairs. Every color of the rainbow. And I get to sort them. It's
super fun. I'd be totally pissed if I wasn't still riding on a high
from my date with Luke. He's already texted me twice. A

heart and an eggplant. I picture his face again, my cheeks heating as I think about last morning. I put a sample in the wrong baggie and have to remove it. Dammit. I need to pay attention. Stupid eggplant emojis distracting me. I sigh.

"Wanna trade?" I ask Seena for the eighth time.

He doesn't even look up from the papers he's shuffling. Some second BFF he is.

Vic one, Louise Grant, was a granny drug dealer with a memory problem. So apparently, the sweet little old lady had notes stashed all around her nap shack. Little scribbles with inventory amounts, nicknames, shipment dates. Whoever let her into their drug ring did not vet her very well first. Or they prioritized her babysitting skills over her secrecy skills. Which stinks. Because that just means that everyone could want to have killed grandma. Her boss, her supplier, her customers.

There was literally so much stuff in that nap shack that Flowers ended up calling out a daytime crew after the wizards and I left. That's where the stashed notes came from. The day team took apart the cribs and searched the papers lining the animal cages. Does it tell you something about how much repetitive tweezer strain I have that I'm begging Seena to switch so I can sort through *that* paperwork?

Even Becca and Petey, two other recruits (who were originally assigned to help with a warrant for a troll who charged with Criminal Accessory for stomping apart a crime scene), have been reassigned to our homicide case. They get to help with the evidence collection. So, four of us are squished basically knee-to-knee in a single cubicle as we work.

Seena might not mind constantly bumping elbows with Becca, seeing as he's dating the cute little sprite, but Petey and I are seriously annoying each other.

"One more time and I swear, I'll drain you, Fox! That was my damn funny bone," Petey grumbles, flashing his vamp fangs at me.

"Didn't seem to make you laugh," I mutter as I stretch my fingers for the sixtieth time. "Besides, me bonking you has still gotta be better than that troll who tried to smash you."

Becca's eyes roll. "That dude wasn't even that huge."

"What was he covering up again?"

She shrugs. "Dunno. Looked like a pit when he was done. But a couple runes weren't smashed. So maybe some kind of magic duel?"

I sigh. "I've always kind of wanted to see an underground duel." My elbow accidentally smacks Petey in the ear as he bends forward.

He curses, "Fucking hell! Are you doing that on purpose? Flowers is right about how annoying—"

"Don't even!" I cut him off. If he finishes that sentence, I might have to punch him in his freckled face. Seriously, bringing in Flowers? That's like the lowest low-down insult you could make. Totally below the belt. I glare at Petey. I used to think he was okay. Now, I'm definitely doubting my previous eval. And I'm not apologizing for that last elbow. If he hadn't bent—

Petey's eyes glow a little red.

Becca tries to break up the tension. "Tell me again about your date with Luke." She yanks on my arm, so I'll face her.

The guys groan, but I smile. "Perfect. It was totally amazing. He's so sweet."

"And *hexy*," Becca fans herself.

Seena clears his throat, "Excuse me?"

She blinks, pulling an innocent face. "What? He's got magical appeal. That's all. No one would ever beat you, Sugar Butt." She winks.

Petey and I burst into laughter.

"Sugar butt, love it!" I repeat.

Seena humphs but turns back to his work. I think his cheeks might turn pink. Becca's in for it later. But she doesn't seem to mind. She tangles their ankles together and bends back over the slime samples she's sorting.

Flowers appears at the cubicle opening and immediately I tense up. I already get to look forward to bleaching the evidence van in the morning, after all the others have gone home. What other torture is the F-bomb gonna give me? (That's the nickname Luke came up with for him yesternight. Isn't it great? I seriously have the best boyfriend in the entire universe.)

"I need some assistance questioning a suspect," Flowers says.

Every hand flies into the air like this is grade school, even mine, though I know there's no chance in hell Flowers is gonna take me if he thinks that this is gonna be important at all.

Flowers takes his time eyeing us. To my shock, he says, "Lyon, come on."

I stand with some difficulty and use Petey's shoulders as a brace so that I can step over Seena and Becca's legs to reach the cubicle opening.

I'm not relieved that Flowers chose me. If anything, it makes me wish for the tweezers more. If Flowers chose me then whatever's coming has got to be bad. What is it? Are we questioning the chickie pups? Or ... shit, did that hippo I lost trample someone? Worst-case scenarios flood my mind.

I vacillate, trying to decide if speaking or allowing the awkward silence keep building would be worse.

Flowers finally breaks the silence. "So, what have you... discovered about reversing your power?"

Shit! He seriously expected me to research that last morning?

I try to stall. "Not much. You want a cup of coffee?" I stride over to Gloria, the well-named office coffeepot, and pour myself a cup from the carafe.

Flowers just narrows his eyes. "Did you even look?" He speaks through his teeth as if it's painful for him. It might be, considering he's carefully selecting every single word he says to avoid his cursed letter.

I can't stop the guilty flush that reddens my cheeks. Damn blonde heritage.

Flowers stalks down the hall toward his office.

"I thought we were questioning a witness," I say as I scurry after him clutching my coffee.

"He can wait a couple minutes," Flowers states as he pushes open the door to his office and strides inside.

I follow tentatively, knowing a lecture's coming. My shoulder start to creep up toward my ears automatically in a defensive hag posture.

"Shut the door."

Shutting the door feels like I'm sealing myself into a tomb. My sense of self-preservation does not like it one bit. I tell her to shut her mouth as I turn to face Flowers.

To my shock, Flowers is calm as he sits on his bouncy ball behind his desk. He doesn't start cursing. Doesn't immediately threaten my life and the lives of my unborn children. He simply takes a huge stack of books and shoves them silently across the desk.

"Here."

"What is this?"

"Research. So you can correct this issue."

I sigh, but I come forward, set down my coffee and bend over the desk in order to grab a stack of books so I can go shove them in my locker.

Flowers stands as I bend over to pull the books toward me.

It's as I'm bent over Flower's desk that Bennett walks in. He doesn't knock, just strides right in and stops dead at the sight of us.

I might have bent from the waist instead of the knees. My face might be near Flowers crotch level because double douche stood. And Flowers hands might possibly look like they're on my boobs from Bennett's angle behind me. Maybe. At least, I assume that's what he thinks he sees when he says—

"What the hell?" Bennett stage whispers as he slams the door behind him. "What's going on?"

Flowers steps back immediately, respectful and at attention. "Lyon and I were just splitting up the research about that issue she caused with my speech last night."

Bennett's eyes flick suspiciously between us.

I move aside and point at the stack of books on the desk. "Flowers was shoving these books over to me."

"Oh," Bennett looks sheepish. "Well, you have a suspect in room two, waiting on questioning."

"Letting him stew a bit, sir," Flowers replies. "Lyon is going to go in and assist."

Bennett scrunches his brow. "I thought it was Becca's turn in the rotation."

"This guy has a -ae, a -airy ... " Flowers eyes shift to tiger briefly.

"A what? A hairy what?" Bennett asks.

"A girl-riend with wings," Flowers hands turn into fists and he presses them into the desk. Probably to resist using those fists on my face.

Bennett looks at me, lost. "A hairy thing with wings? A Griffin? A genfin?" Bennett asks, clearly not understanding Flowers at all.

"GIRL-riend," Flowers repeats. Whatever I did to him, his lips won't even form the 'f' sound at all.

"Girl rent? He rents from a girl? Rents girls? He's into prostitution? Fuck. Write it down man. I have no clue."

But Flowers can't write it down because he's so pissed, his hands have shifted into tiger paws.

I close my eyes and clench my teeth as I translate for Flowers. "He means fairy girlfriend. This suspect has a fairy girlfriend. He wants me in the room to try and soften the guy up." My eyes apologize to Flowers but he simply points a paw at the stack of books. I nod. FML and my powers.

Bennett purses his lips like he doesn't like the idea of me softening anyone up. Hey, I don't really either, especially considering the guy we're about to question is probably one of the addicts from the nap shack last night. Given the state of the shack, I'm sure this guy's hygiene level is questionable at best. I hope it isn't the chickie pup. Because, seriously, if he asked me out and had a girlfriend, we will be having words.

"Alright. Just make sure Becca gets the next one," Bennett says.

Flowers gives a brisk nod. "Yes, sir."

Bennett strides out, deliberately leaving Flower's office door wide open. He makes eye contact with Flowers that is almost dad-like. As in 'keep this door open young man.'

I fight an eye roll. Not an issue. Unless he worries Flowers will kill me. Then—very much an issue.

"Who are we going to question?" I ask as I heft the stack of books into my arms.

"Remember that little shit lizard bear that lost his tail?"

"Him?"

Flowers nods. "Seena saw him on the list o- people who owe money to Louise Grant about an hour ago. He's about two thousand gold in the hole."

"Got it. Am I playing good cop?"

Flowers rolls his eyes. "Obviously. Put those books away, grab the guy a co—ee... a drink, and meet me in two. And don't -uck this up." Flowers shakes out his paws and they transform back to human. He stands and walks out of the room without offering to help me carry the fifty pounds of books he loaded me down with, like the troll fart he is.

I decide I'm going to start making all my curse words tiger-related. Because I can't think of anything worse than that tiger. So, when I load the books into my locker and one hits my foot, what do I say? "Striped shifters—that hurt!"

When I limp into questioning after pulling every muscle in my back, I stop short. The lizard bear's human form is not at all what I expect. His look screams nerdy accountant. He's got thinning hair on top, thick glasses, he's slightly on the chubby side. His arms are covered in thick black hair that I'm sure he wishes were on his head on a daily basis. (I'm telling you, that arm hair is so thick, it'd make a seriously nice toupee.) He doesn't look capable of murder to me. At least not for two large. But I have a role to play, so I slide into my chair with a smile. I push a steaming cup of joe toward him.

Lizard bear smiles and takes the coffee gratefully. I finally learn his name when Flowers says, "Mr. Geraldo Lilypunt, thanks -or coming down to talk to us. I'm hoping we can come to a mutually beneshicial arrangement."

I press my lips together. Flowers totally just gave himself a lisp so he could get that word out. Is the recorder on in here? Oh God, I hope so. I need to replay that endlessly for Seena and JR. Endlessly.

Mr. Lilypunt gives a brief nod, but Flowers says, "I need you to verbally agree, sir."

"Yes," Lilypunt hisses and I can hear a bit of lizard in his voice. It has a hissy, breathy quality.

"So, tell us about last night," Flowers crosses his arms and leans against the wall. He lets the silence stretch.

Lilypunt's fingers dance nervously over the sides of the coffee cup. "Look, I don't know what you want me to say. Last night was crazy. Okay?"

"Start at the beginning. When you arrived at the nap shack, what did you see?"

Lilypunt swipes at the sweat beading on his forehead. He takes a sip of coffee. "I dunno. It was dark."

"Not gonna buy that," Flowers says.

Lilypunt growls and gnashes his teeth. I'm a little surprised by that response. He seems like such a nerd. But I guess there is a bit of bear in him somewhere. He turns the growl into clearing his throat and apologizes.

"So sorry about that. Tired." He takes a long drink of coffee.

I go for a soft smile and lean forward, hoping to put him at ease. "We really appreciate you coming in. We're just trying to figure out what happened to that poor caretaker." See how tactful that was? How I said caretaker, not drug dealer?

"Louise? Something happened to Louise?" Lilypunt shifts in his seat, agitated. His fingers grab the edge of the table, then he retracts them. His eyes flicker between Flowers and me. "What happened to her? Is she okay?"

I can't quite figure this guy out. He was just growling and now he's acting scared as shit. I'm glad I'm not dealing with him alone because he seems unbalanced.

I give him a pitying look, as if he's just a victim. "What can you tell me about Louise?"

Lilypunt shrugs, "She's nice. Always has a smile … you know, when I'd see her at the grocery store or something," Lilypunt backtracks, realizing he might have just made himself look like a regular. (Yeah, sorry buddy, your actions are already kinda doing that.)

"Last time you saw her, she say anything?" Flowers asks.

Lilypunt shakes his head. "She was arguing with some girl when I came in—about a bill or something."

I smile and nod to encourage him. (I'm semi-shocked he might have dropped useful information.) "What did this girl look like?"

"Tall. Really tall."

"Hair color?"

"Pink maybe? Orange? Like I said, it was dark."

"What'd she say?"

Lilypunt shakes his head as he recalls, "She was really angry, saying stuff like Louise did that on purpose—Louise was yelling right back at her saying about what happened to the bill wasn't her fault or something—"

"What was on purpose?" I lean forward. It sounds like Lilypunt could have witnessed someone with a motive to kill Louise.

"When women argue, I just get out of the way," Lilypunt holds up his hands.

I glance over at Flowers to see him nodding and I have to resist rolling my eyes.

I change the subject. "Tell me more about this girl. Had you seen her around there before?"

Lilypunt shrugs. "All those young kids look the same to me. Black clothes and chains and all that."

"Any defining features? Big nose? Tattoos?"

Lilypunt rubs his face and sighs. He yawns and rests his head on his hand. His eyelids look heavy. "Don't they all have tattoos?"

"What were the tattoos of?" I ask.

He shrugs and yawns again. "I just saw a couple letters on her neck, that's all."

"What did it say?"

"I don't know. Just a couple letters. Her initials. E.W. or something."

"Think you could recognize her if you saw her again?"

He shrugs.

Great. Lizard bear apparently got the lizard brain. I rate his helpfulness as a negative four. Louise had scattered notes about money all over the place. A lot of people owed her. And whatever this kid owed her; it couldn't be more than Lilypunt.

I turn to Flowers who just continues to lean unhelpfully against the wall. I wonder if he knew how utterly useless this interview was going to be and if he's just torturing me with it.

He jerks his head toward the witness as if to say, 'get on with it.'

I turn back to Lilypunt to find him nodding off with his hand for a pillow.

Flowers says, "Nearly hibernation season. Wake him up."

I swallow a sigh. Freaking bear shifters. "Sir. Sir!" I smack the table to wake him up. Lilypunt jumps. His knees smack the table, sending the cup of coffee tumbling to the floor as he leaps backwards and grabs onto the side wall. His hands shift into furry claws and he scurries up the cinderblock wall a few feet before he realizes that he's not in danger.

"Care to join me back at the table?" I ask patiently, though I really feel like calling out a psychoanimalist. This guy's shifter side has way more control over his instincts than normal. I keep a fake smile on my face as I wait for Lilypunt to climb back down the wall, shift his hands back to normal, and sit. It takes him a few minutes.

While I wait, I silently give myself a patience award, frame it, and set it on my imaginary desk. It's got one of those gold embossed stickers on it and everything. Finally—it feels like two years later—I continue questioning the suspect, "Louise have any family?"

"Um a son or something … she mighta' mentioned him helping her out a few times. Guess there's a hippo she knows that gets a little rough. Her son was the muscle for that, I think."

Flowers and I exchange a look. I don't know if he ever sent someone after that hippo I lost yesternight. I didn't hear about a rampage on the evening news. So, I hope we're good. Hopefully this rough hippo is cooling his jets at home and not rampaging through the town.

"Know anything else about her son?" I ask, since Flowers doesn't seem too eager to jump into the conversation.

"Never met him myself, but everyone there always said he was a bit of an ass."

"He get along with his mom?"

Lilypunt shrugs. "Not sure. I think he works at a bookstore: Tall Tales, maybe?"

Darn it all. I love Tall Tales. Hopefully, her son doesn't work there. I don't want to taint my memories of my favorite bookstore. "Anything else?"

Lilypunt shakes his head. "Didn't have too much time to talk to her ever. Just casual chats. Weekend. Weather. That kinda thing."

"Do you know the son's name?" I ask.

"Fred or Freddie or something?" Lilypunt runs a hand through his hair.

I nod. "Great. Great." Dammit all to hell. Why does the son have to have an 'f' name? I turn to Flowers.

He stands up from where's he's slouched. He makes eye contact with Lilypunt as he asks, "How many times a week do you typically use Nappies?"

Lilypunt pales. "What? I don't. It's was a one-time—"

Flower's glare makes Lilypunt rethink his lie.

"Once in a great while," he says. "That's it. I swear."

"Who else do you know there? Anyone you regularly go with?"

"No," Lilypunt's headshake gets a bit more frantic. "Nope. Solo thing."

"How did you pay for your Nappies?" I jump in.

"I really, I swear. I don't use that much! I don't!" Lilypunt sweat gets worse. And then his eyes flash. His hands start to shake. I see scales and fur start to sprout along his neck.

Crap. He's avoiding the question and he's about to meltdown. He looks like he's on the edge of losing his temper and shifting in public.

I turn to Flowers, who doesn't seem at all bothered. In fact, Flowers swaggers forward.

"Really? Don't use much?" He slams something onto the table in front of me. "Then explain this receipt that was in your wallet! Explain why you just bought an entire *case* o-diapers!"

"My girl's pregnant," the hiss in Lilypunt's voice gets more pronounced. A lizard tongue flicks out of his mouth and his nails start to lengthen into claws.

"No, she's not. Spoke with her earlier," Flowers retorts, leaning over the table. "Those diapers were yours. You know it. I know it. You want your girl to know it? How you like to shit in these stink bags and cry in some old lady's arms?"

Lilypunt's eyes widen. Then he slumps forward in his seat and holds his head in his hands.

"I'm gonna let you think a bit. Then we'll come back and talk about how much money you owed Louise."

Lilypunt puts his head on the table. "I think I want a lawyer."

Flowers growls. "Oh, you're gonna need one."

He leads the way out. I scoop up the receipt and follow, scanning the list of purchases until I see it: Haggies Overnights, 24 pack.

Damn. Doomed by diapers.

9

The rest of the work night is uneventful.

I'm marching down to the parking garage to spray our van down with every kind of swamp-ass repellent I can find. My arms are loaded with buckets full of spray bottles and rags and paper towels.

I push open the door to the parking garage with my butt and nearly brain Tabby, who's about to pull the handle on the other side. Right behind her is Sarah Snow, who's dressed like she's going to a funeral. In fact, my eyes roam over Tabby again. Both ladies are looking particularly professional. They're wearing black suits. Sarah's looks velvet and she has a sharp purple blouse underneath. Tabby's is so high waisted it could be from the seventies. It might actually be from the seventies. I don't think I've ever seen her look so dressed up. Not even when I met her … in court.

I swallow a sigh and look down at Tabby. "Did you get arrested again?"

"No!" she says indignantly, shaking her head and making her white curls bounce. "We're here on business."

I set down my buckets of cleaning supplies and block the door. My fairy senses are tingling on this one. "What kind of business?" I cross my arms. Please don't say matchmaking. Please don't.

"We're here to meet with a client," Sarah's tone is evasive.

That sets off alarm bells in my brain. "What kind of client? A client that's hired you?" I press. No way in hell am I letting them through the door if they're going to harass Flowers.

"He will," Sarah crosses her arms defiantly.

"No, please. I told you anyone but him."

The door smacks me in the back, and I fall to my knees on the concrete. "Son of a Bengel!" I curse as my hands scrape the concrete.

Behind me, Petey's voice asks, "What are you doing blocking the door, Fox?"

I grumble and pull myself to my knees. "I'm trying to stop these two—" But when I look up, the two members of Blue Snow Matchmaking are gone.

"Sabertooth balls," I mutter. Those women are gonna get me fired.

"What did you say?"

"I've decided all curse words should be tiger-related."

Petey's eyes grow wide. "If Flowers ever finds out—"

I lean closer to Petey and say, "You know he's the type to kill the messenger, right?"

Petey waves his hands. "Whoa! I'm not gonna tell him!" (Sometimes I wonder how he became a vamp. He doesn't fit the badass MO at all.)

"Good. Now come with me." I yank open the door to the building.

"Um … I was heading home."

I raise an eyebrow. "You let those women in. You're gonna have to help me get them out."

Petey's boyish face is confused. He runs a hand through his auburn hair. It's his nervous tell. "Are they gonna attack someone in there?"

"Worse," I whisper, letting him fester a second. "They're gonna try and set up Flowers. On a date."

Petey's eyes widen and he takes a step backward, toward the parking garage. "Wait. You just said he'll kill the messenger."

"If they make it up there, I'm telling him you let them in."

Petey darts past me into the stairwell. He uses vamp speed, so he's basically a blur with a streak of red on top.

I smile and give myself an internal high-five. Then I start up the stairs and text Becca.

Code Kitty. I repeat Code Kitty.

Now? She responds.

They're on their way up the stairs.

During our hours of evidence bagging, when the guys were gone for their turn sitting in on questioning (they got stuck with chickie pups), I briefed her on the whole Blue Snow debacle. Hopefully, she can run interference.

Luckily for us all, Petey is faster than two old ladies. He has them stopped on the stairwell, just in front of the door that leads to the first floor of the courthouse and our lovely investigative offices.

"I'm sorry, but you need a badge to go in there," Petey crosses his arms. "Otherwise you need to use the public entrance out front."

He actually sounds good. All official and shit. I start to creep back down the stairs. No need to let them know I put him up to this.

But Sarah spots me. "Lyon Fox! You get your tush up here and tell this young man we're with you."

I turn, straddling two steps. "But … you're not with me."

Sarah's eyes narrow. "Oh really? I suppose that apricot strudel I made is just gonna have to go—"

"Not fair!" I snap. She's bribing me with sweets? She knows my fae Achilles' heel. "I told you not to use my boss for—"

"We aren't using him," Tabby snaps. "We're getting his help."

"We've already called him, and he agreed last morning—"

I smack a hand to my forehead. I look around for a minute, wondering if Gor the goblin is anywhere in the vicinity. He had a way of making me feel like I'd stepped into my worst nightmare. I'm pretty sure that's what's happened. This is my worst nightmare.

Unless … this is all a joke. That has to be it. These women are playing a joke on me. "I'm not on 'Stake Out' am I?" I ask, peering behind me for hidden cameras. The vamp prank show has recently gone viral and their videos are popping up everywhere online. Vamps who prank supernaturals. Only three have died so far. Twenty pranks. Pretty impressive stats. If it wasn't vamps running the pranks, I'd totally kill whoever's pranking me now. I smile for the hidden cameras. "Okay. I get it. Joke's on me."

Everyone else on the stairs just keeps glaring at me.

Dammit.

I don't want this to be real.

I stomp my foot. "You can't go in there and set up my boss on a date!"

The door swings open behind Petey. And who's there?

Bennett. Of course. He has to witness every humiliating moment of my life. Next to him is none other than Diego Flores.

Sarah and Tabby immediately grin. Tabby gets this overly self-satisfied, cat-who-got-the-cream grin. And Sarah just holds out a hand like a debutante. Or a princess. "Why, just the gentleman we were hoping to see."

"Me?" Bennett touches his chest, confused.

"Well, if you want a date, then sure," Tabby says.

"They're actually here -or me," Flowers grins and punches Bennett on the shoulder. "But maybe I'll see some girl who'll match you, Boss."

My eyes widen. "What?!"

Flowers is smiling. Again. I swear Gor the Goblin's got to be messing with me. Flowers smiling—it's not supposed to happen. It's just not. It's unnatural.

Bennett looks a little pleased by my shock, thinking I'm indignant about him dating. Which—yeah, I would be. Because I'm selfish like that. But right now, I'm really just reeling from this entire situation. What the hell is going on?

Somehow, Tabby and Sarah convinced Flowers that he should go along with this matchmaking scheme. Has the apocalypse started? I mean, I know I saw stars over at Luke's place last night. But I didn't think it was literally world-ending stuff. I was just stroking the man's ego when I said that. (I mean, it was toe-curlingly good.) Ah, crap. I really gotta watch what I say. Did I somehow cause the universe to collapse? Shit!

Flowers smirks at all of us and says, "You're looking at the new director o- matching at Blue Snow Matchmaking."

Bennett turns and gives Flowers a disbelieving stare. "You're doing what?"

Flowers gloats a bit. "I get to vet all the women. Make sure any crazies don't make it through. It's a hard job, man, but someone's ..."

Bennett thumps him on the back, thankfully cutting off what was sure to be an unoriginal arrogant-ass monologue. "Good luck, man."

Flowers gives one of those weird male chin raises. The 'yeah' or 'I'll see you' ones. Then he trots down the stairs and extends his elbows to my neighbor and her best friend so they can loop their arms through his. "Ladies," he says to Sarah and Tabby, "can I escort you down to the car?"

Damn. Those women are smart as shit. They just locked Flores into blind dates of their choice and he doesn't even realize it. Holy rabid frothing tigers. They might just be the most manipulative, reaper-level, badass matchmakers of all time. My urge to beat them morphs into the urge to *be* them.

Sarah demurely takes Flower's arm. Tabby waves him off, muttering about antiquated gestures.

Sarah giggles at her clueless escort. "We've already gotten an applicant. A sweet young thing. Mid-twenties. Kind of shy. Think you could interview her at Wendel's?"

Sarah and Flowers walk down past me. Tabby follows shortly after. I'm starstruck. I think we all are a little stunned. Petey, Bennett, and I exchange a look.

"Did that really just happen?" Bennett asks.

"Oh, it happened," Petey runs a hand through his hair. "I'm just kinda wondering if I'm dead all over again, this time in another dimension."

I turn and stare at the door to the parking garage for a second. "I'm still supposed to bleach the police van. But I really … really need to see this go down."

A second later, Bennett and Petey are on my heels. Bennett holds out his hand for the van keys. "I'll drive while you clean."

Petey says, "I'll help you clean on the way if you'll let me watch, too."

An evil, excited grin spreads across my face. "Let's go watch this puss—" I can't finish the word. Dammit.

"Pussy cat," Bennett supplies.

"Thank you—get his date on."

We all rush out the door.

I have a feeling these dates are gonna be epic. They're gonna blow like Vesuvius. They're gonna be *cat*-astrophic.

And if I have my way, they're getting posted on BooTube.

NEVER BLEACH A VAN WHILE A DRAGON DRIVES. THEY'RE HOT-headed by nature. Bennett's road rage is fierce. Let's just say it's a good thing Petey's already undead, otherwise the bleach bucket he took to the face mighta' been a problem. As it is, he just reeks so much he can't go inside.

He mumbles curses under his breath because he can't exactly berate Bennett out loud. That would be career suicide. He hides in the bushes near the windows, trying to peer in as he airs out. Since it's near dawn, he's gonna have to move around as the sun rises so he doesn't get burnt.

I pat his back. "I brought my phone. I'll do what I can to get footage if you need to leave."

I don't see Bennett after I get Petey set up, so I go to the side door to an employee entrance and walk in like I own the place. Employees give me the side eye as I walk through the kitchen, but I just make my way over to Cherry Jones, the unicorn shifter who runs the joint.

"Hey lady, mind if I do some covert ops?"

Cherry's stirring up a berry and fisheye pie filling at the moment, and the blue ooze smells like heaven, even if the blinking is a bit disconcerting. She stops stirring and wipes an arm across her pale forehead, pushing back her rainbow-colored locks of hair. "Is this gonna wreck my dining room?"

When I explain the sneaky nature of my elderly friends, Cherry bursts into laughter. "Damn! That's awesome! What do you need from me?"

"I was wondering if one of your servers could 'drop my phone' under the table and let it record their convo while I watch your security feed. Pretty please?"

She shakes her head and laughs. "Tara!" she calls a waitress over. "Help my friend Ly-ly out."

I get all set up in the security room and I'm feeling a little bit smug when I lean over and see Flowers grabbing some napkins and heading to one of the fifties style diner booths, where a woman waits. Right behind him is Bennett, who slides into the very next booth with a burger, acting like he's out to dinner alone.

Crap. Why didn't I just do that? I'm an idiot.

But my waitress is already in motion. Tara's actually a great super-spy buddy. She 'drops' my phone on the floor, kicks it under the booth, and heads back toward me. And then she sits down next to me and flicks out an earbud, tossing it to me.

"I had your phone call my phone. My phone's recording the call. And then I told Cherry I'm taking a break."

Instant gratification washes over me as I hear Flowers trying to make small talk.

"So, Mrs. Snow tells me you like mountain climbing?" It's so totally weird to hear him try to make friendly conversation. If I weren't watching him on the screen at the same time, I'd swear it wasn't Flowers talking. He's using a tone of voice that I've literally never heard from him before. He almost sounds normal.

The girl mumbles her response, like she's super shy. I barely hear her say, "Yes."

"What made you get into mountain climbing?"

"I grew up in the mountains," the girl hides behind a head of sparkling, straight white hair. I can hardly make out her face, except for a button nose.

"Really? Where? I go hiking around here a lot," I can already hear impatient Flowers bubbling right underneath the surface. Ooh, is he gonna be able to stay nice? Or is his rude gonna show?

I lean in. This is as addicting as reality TV.

"I'm not from around here."

"Okay," Flowers bites into his burger and chews, letting the awkward stretch out and get nice and thick. Because the girl doesn't offer up any more info. She just sits there, playing with her fries, still hiding her face.

Flowers sighs and puts his burger down. "Look, Babie, you want to date, right? Then you need to speak up a little more. Give more in-ormation… I mean, talk more about yourself."

"Okay," Babie slouches a bit.

"Things like where you were born. Or grew up."

"Nepal."

"More than one word answers, Babie."

"I'm from Nepal."

Flowers grits his teeth. I kinda feel sorry for this poor girl. Where did Sarah and Tabby dig her up? She's clearly not ready to date. And Flowers is clearly not a match for her. I rethink my earlier praise for Blue Snow. I think they mightta' missed the mark with this one.

"I'm … I was born right here in Tres Lunas," Flowers replies. I realize he changed his sentence to avoid the word 'from.' His statement gets no response from Babie so he tries again. "So, what made you leave Nepal?"

"Hunters," Babie takes the world's smallest bite of a fry. So small she can swallow it whole. Without chewing. The kind of bite supermodels take before they go gorge on spinach. I might be reclassifying her from the pitiful to the plain weird category. Who doesn't like fries?

"One word answer again, Babie," Flowers scolds, though far more gently than he'd ever scold me.

"Sorry. Hunters made me leave."

The look on his face makes me wish I could freeze frame the security footage. I'm pretty sure it's the same look he gives me six times a day. Utter frustration. He does this thing where his teeth show. It might be a growly tiger thing. But it's kinda funny. Very comic book. And it really just makes me wanna irritate him more to see it again.

Babie doesn't take it that way. "Did you just show your teeth to me?" she asks, uttering her first full sentence since they sat down. She pushes her hair back from her face and bares her own teeth. Her canines elongate. Her eyes get a slightly reddish glow.

Flowers sits back in his seat, stunned.

I'm stunned as she actually repeats her sentence. Unprompted.

"I said, did you just show your teeth to me?!" This time she growls as she leans forward over the table. The red glow in her eyes intensifies. And suddenly, she shifts. In public.

Her clothes shred. She grows three feet taller, tipping the table and the food toward Flowers. White hair sprouts all over her body and her hands turn into big, clawed monstrosities.

"Burning tiger tails!" I whisper. Blue Snow Matchmaking set Flowers up with a yeti!

10

Bennett and Flowers are way too casual as they arrest poor Babie for public shifting. I sneak out of the security room and collect my phone while they're hustling the raging mountain monster outside and into the van, still growling about Flower's teeth.

All in all, the date went way worse than I was expecting, but the arrest went far better, mainly because Bennett was there, and I didn't have to help. (What? Self-preservation. When Babie shifted her feet grew until they were two feet long. She woulda' crushed me. Only Bennett's mini blowtorch mouth kept her from rampaging and destroying the place.)

I pocket my phone, wondering how I'm gonna tell Sarah and Tabby about this disaster (hoping Babie isn't one of their friends' granddaughters or something). I absentmindedly steal a handful of Bennett's fries from his abandoned meal on the table.

When I turn around, he's watching me, arms crossed and a bemused smirk on his face. It's far better than the haunted look he wore earlier this evening. If torturing Flowers with bad dates helps put Bennett in a better mood, I'll take it.

"You missed all the drama," Bennett says. "You stay outside with Petey?"

I shrug. "Saw it on the security cameras."

He rolls his eyes up to the ceiling. "Don't tell me any more. I don't want to know. If you were doing anything even slightly legally grey, I don't wanna know."

I shrug and shove another fry in my mouth. Fine. I won't tell him I was listening/recording on my phone. It's more for my friends' benefit anyway. "Did you see the way she ate fries? Just from that, I could tell she was crazy."

Bennett's grin turns into a laugh. "Have to admit, that was a more exciting dinner than I'm used to."

"Are all shifters that crazy? I feel like that's all I've run into lately."

Ben shrugs. "You're dealing with drugs on this case. They mess up mental and magical connections."

I sigh, "Yeah, that's true."

Bennett lowers his voice. "Mixed shifters also have it harder from the get-go. I mean, my dragon tugs at me. But what if I was a dragon deer? What if half of me was literally the prey of the other half? That can mess you up big time. Mentally, half of you wants to destroy the other half." He shakes his head. "I can see why so many of these poor mixed shifters get hooked. Not to mention their looks. Mixed shifters generally look like both of their parents, literally. So, if a woman's dad was a lion shifter, she gets a mane when she shifts. Peacock—tail feathers. Same for guys. Even without the predator-prey mental issues, that can mess you up."

Those are good points.

He grabs his burger and shoves it into a to-go box. Then he pulls out a second box, tosses his fries in it and hands the box to me. Ben pulls a honey packet from his pocket and tosses that to me, too.

I can't help the slightly mushy feeling that gives me. He's always been a thoughtful guy. But then Luke pops into my head and I shove that mushy feeling away with a, "Thanks, Boss."

He gives me a sad smile. "Sure thing."

We leave Wendel's in silence. I end up squished between Bennett and Petey on the van's bench seat for the ride back to the station. Babie is stuffed in the back. She's gone human and shy again.

My knee accidentally rubs against Bennett's and I see his fists clench on the steering wheel. I don't think my knee touching a guy's knee has been this awkward and wrought with sexual tension since I was twelve and we went on a field trip to the zombie war re-enactment. (Note: When I become a museum director in another life, I will not hire actual zombies to re-enact the war. At least two kids in that class got left behind on the field muttering "brains.") I try to ignore the awkwardness by eating my fries, but end up spilling honey on my uniform, which is just great since I'm already down that uniform from the nap shack.

When we get to the station, Bennett has a rookie start booking the yeti. Flowers gives a statement, then comes over to Petey and me.

"I need to thollow up on the son oth our vic, Thread Grant."

He just lisped through that whole sentence. Thread for Fred is epic. I bite my lip and keep my face neutral.

It doesn't work. Flowers can sense my amusement. He gives me a threatening glare as Petey just looks confused by the lisp thing.

"I thought his name was Fred."

"Yup. That's what I said."

I press my lips together hard and keep quiet, avoiding eye contact. I have no doubt that after a yeti just blew up on him, Flowers has some anger to vent. I don't need to be vented on.

"What can I do to help, sir?" Petey opts to be a kiss ass.

Flowers looks frustrated when we don't give him an outlet for his rage, but he holds it in because we're in public, cops and people under arrest swarming all around. He continues, "I called Tall Tales and it looks like Grant's working now. You two, come on."

We're supposed to clock out, but crime doesn't sleep. Besides, I'm pretty sure Flowers doesn't want to have to lisp in front of the general public, which would definitely happen if he had to say "Fred" multiple times. I bite back a sigh and nod. Guess I'll just have to put off researching a cure for this 'effing' curse until later. Heartbreaking.

We get to Tall Tales just as story-time ends. The place is flooded with kids. Little snotty-nosed witches run around as their mothers stare blankly off into space holding coffee cups. A mother genie grabs her toddler and stuffs him back into his lamp as he throws a tantrum.

We avoid the audioboos section, where a number of bored ghosts float, waiting for customers. You can hire them to follow you around and read a book to you. But the last time I did that, I got an asshole named Brian who kept ruining the sex scenes by blowing raspberries or adding a running commentary on how particular positions weren't physically possible. I'm pretty sure his wife killed him and he's bitter about it. Anyway, I haven't gotten an audioboo since.

It turns out that "Freddie" works in the stockroom, per the manager. When we enter, he's doing donuts in the forklift.

"This is gonna go well," I say.

Petey snorts.

Flowers jerks his head and stares at me. At first, I'm not sure what he wants. But then I realize.

"Fred Grant!" I call out.

The donuts slowly stop. Freddie turns to us and pulls off his safety goggles. I love the irony of that. Wearing safety goggles as he does dangerous spins in his forklift. I have a feeling he's a dead-to-rights idiot. My feeling is not wrong.

"Whas' up?" Freddie trots over, his hair flopping in his eyes. He does that annoying emo headshake thing to get the hair out of his eyes, instead of just using his hand to move it like a normal person. He's a skinny dude, with one of those Adam's apples that protrudes so much it looks like it hurts.

"I'm sorry. Your mom passed away," I tell him.

Freddie doesn't look very surprised. Maybe the ME's office told him. I'm not too clear on the protocol of that yet. We haven't gotten that far in the grandiose booklet that is the Tres Lunas Investigative Training Manual. (The evil thing is five inches thick. But does the government pay for a real binding? Nope. Those cheap asses pay for those plastic spines with claw tabs that pop the eff off every time you turn a page.)

I turn to Flowers. This isn't my first murder. But it is kinda the first time I'm officially allowed to talk. And I don't know what to say.

Flowers turns to Freddie. "When did you see your mom last?"

Freddie scratches his head. "Um … two days ago? Was that Tuesday? She always makes meatloaf on Tuesdays."

"You go over on Tuesday?"

"Go over?" Freddie looks lost.

"To her house?" Flowers clarifies.

"Ummm … nah. I'm kinda in between places right now."

Ah. Another millennial who lives with his mom. Like, I know I'm technically millennial. But I don't get it. Maybe it's because my mother's such a nightmare. But who wouldn't want their independence? Apparently, Freddie, who likes meatloaf.

"You and your mom get along?" I ask, adding a smile and a, "I couldn't stand my mom."

"She wasn't home much."

"Worked a lot?"

He nods.

"Freddie, who's your mom's boss?" I ask.

Flowers glares at me. Apparently, I'm supposed to be good at questioning. Not direct.

Freddie shrugs and says, "Dunno."

Petey leans forward, his voice smooth and seductive. He puts off a vampire predator pheromone or something that sends chills down my spine. "You never met him?" Petey asks.

Freddie gulps.

"No. She wouldn't let me meet him."

"So her boss was a man," Petey leans forward, letting his fangs extend slightly.

"Um … Um…"

"You will tell me the truth," Petey commands.

"Yes." Freddie's voice is suddenly woozy and he sways on his feet. Petey's doing a number on him. For the millionth time in my life I wish I was not a super-loser. I wish I had useful, cool powers like Petey. Dammit!

Petey puts out his hand and holds Freddie by the shoulder. "Her boss's name?"

"Tar."

"Tar what?"

"Just Tar."

Tar is a troll name. Freddie might have just tied this drug operation to the troll gang, the Bloods. I mean, Flowers suspected it before. And we have lots of evidence that might tie it to them. But this is quicker.

Petey looks back to Flowers, who gives an approving head nod. Frickin' tiger feces! Guess Petey just got moved up to class favorite. Stupid vampire powers. If I had compulsion as a power, I coulda' done that, too. Eff the universe.

I try asking a question anyway, because there's a stupid part of me that doesn't know when it's time to shut up. That part says, "So, this was a Blood operation?"

"Whoa!" Freddie takes a few steps back. "I don't wanna get smashed. I dunno anything about them. I dunno what you're talking about. She's never said anything about a gang."

"If it was a Blood operation, they usually hand down positions to children. Wouldn't you inherit the nap shack?" I ask.

Freddie crinkles his nose. "You think I wanna wipe poopy butts all night? No thanks."

Flowers pretty much crushes my bicep when he yanks me back. "Sorry, Mr. Grant. This is our trainee. She doesn't know anything about anything yet."

Fred eyes me warily, but he nods at Flowers. "I had a trainee a couple months back. Couldn't hack it." He jerks his head at the shelves. "Guy lied on his application. He was a phoenix shifter. Can you imagine a phoenix working in a bookstore? Idiot. Burned two pallets of books in a row."

Flowers gives a sympathetic nod. "That uncontrolled shitting is the worst."

I bite my lip and turn away. I can't even. Flowers just said shitting instead of shifting. *Uncontrolled* shitting. Gah—that is comic gold right there. I'm gonna be so sad when I figure out how to reverse this effing problem.

"Yeah, I felt bad for the guy before we fired him. Girlfriend moved away for grad school or something. But, dude. This is serious stuff. Can't go losing your head and get all heartbroken up in here. Not when you're a walking firestick."

I'm finally able to turn around after swallowing my giggles.

Flowers is nodding at Freddie. "Mr. Grant, I just have one last question." He leans forward. "What kind of creature was your mom?"

"What?" Freddie looks nervous. He looks side to side, though there's no one else in the warehouse with us. "What do you mean?"

Flowers looks almost regretful when he says, "Mr. Grant, most Nappie dealers were once users. Nappies tend to attract certain types of shithters."

Aw, man. I'm kinda disappointed he lisped it this time.

Freddie shakes his head. "I dunno what you're talking about. She was a witch. I'm a wizard. That's it."

Petey leans in and blasts Freddie with compulsion again. "We aren't here to hurt you, Fred. We're here to help you. We just need to know so we can do our job. We want to find out who hurt your mom."

Freddie looks a little dazed as he whispers, "She was a baboon-bird."

Immediately, I'm assaulted with images from *The Wizard of Oz*. It seems fitting that the drug-dealing granny was a flying monkey.

Flowers nods and claps Freddie on the shoulder. "I'll be in touch. I'm sure more questions will come up. But, thanks."

Freddie trots after us. "You aren't gonna like, release that info, right? About her shifter animal?"

Flowers turns. "I wasn't planning on it. Why?"

Freddie looks down at his shoes. "Because, I kinda told everyone here I'm just a sucky wizard."

Looks like the phoenix wasn't the only one who lied on his job application. Sad thing is, if I lived across the Veil, I'd probably lie about my heritage if I could, too. Over there, it's better to be a kidnapped human baby raised by fairies than a fairy with no powers. Of course, the blue stone in my chin is a dead giveaway. I never could have lied like Freddie. I feel bad for the baboon-bird, emo dude.

It's no fun being a freak.

11

After Tall Tales, I'm finally done. I'm too tired and lazy to go back to the office and pick up all my spare clothes and that pile of books. I'm too tired to go to the dry cleaners and get my uniform back. I just want to eat and crash.

I text Luke, with little hope that I'll see him because the sun's up now. That's probably a good thing though, because if I did see him, there's little hope that I would actually sleep.

Then I call JR, who sounds like she's in the middle of dinner.

"Hello?" she mumbles with her mouth full.

"Ugh. I'm starving. What are you eating?" I ask.

"Come over. Danny made stir fry."

"Vegetables?" Suddenly, my appetite goes way down.

"We have sweet and sour sauce," she replies.

"I'm there." I hang up and get a Broomer over to her place.

JR lives in one of those tiny converted garage apartments in a semi-decent part of town. They call her place a studio but it's really like the cupboard under the stairs. Tiny. A bathroom is stuck over in one corner with nothing but a curtain rod and some of JR's plant babies to give you privacy. There's a tiny countertop with a two-burner stovetop and a microwave that doesn't work. I'm always on JR to tell her landlord to get that fixed, but she doesn't want him coming into her place. Her landlord is a ghost. And since she's a nymph, her place is a tangle of vines and flowering plants. He'd slime the whole thing with ectoplasm.

Danny trots over on his satyr hooves and hands me a bowl of stir fry and the squirt bottle of sweet and sour. I sit down on a stump. JR waves a hand and a frond with giant leaves leans over and becomes my backrest. She and Danny snuggle up on a fallen log she calls her love seat. She starts stroking the goat horns that pop up out of his curly black hair. He eats while JR peppers me with questions about Luke.

"Brothers and sisters?"

"None that made the change."

"Hobbies?"

"Reading and a weird one—don't laugh—element collection."

Both Danny and JR give me odd looks.

"What the heck is that?" Danny asks.

"It's a science thing. It's literally going around town trying to collect the periodic elements from everynight items."

"That's a thing?"

"Apparently, this is the International Year of the Periodic Table," I recite.

"Says who?"

"I dunno. People. He said something about a one-hundred-fifty-year anniversary or something," I shrug as I squirt a ton of sweet and sour sauce onto my fork to drown out the taste of broccoli. I take a bite. Tolerable. The sauce makes it just tolerable.

"Okay. Still lost. What the hell is element collection? How is that a hobby?" JR stops stroking Danny's horns and he gives a little bleat.

I finish my bite and explain, "So, he has a list of things he's looking for that contain different elements. He's doing two tables. A supernatural version and a human version. And he goes around town looking for things on his lists. He collects them and puts them into a shadow box in the shape of the periodic table."

JR smiles and rolls her eyes. "That's so nerdy."

Danny disagrees, "Nah, that's awesome. What's the weirdest thing he's got?"

"OMG. Sulfur from a dragon's breath in a vial. Calcium off a mermaid's scales. Neon from a will-o'-the-wisp. A kinda cool human one was a computer chip for gold. But a lot of the others ... there was something about cobalt and lithium ion batteries before I distracted him."

"Wow. Sounds like we will not be going on a double date any time soon," JR laughs, "I might fall asleep. Does he lose hot points for this or gain smart points?"

I flick a pea pod from my bowl at her. "Not nice."

"I just don't know a guy that hot that's into that stuff. How does that happen?"

Danny puts his hand around her, "Babe, not cool. Maybe he wasn't hot as a kid."

JR gives him a look. "He's like a supermodel. No way that's possible."

Danny just rolls his eyes. "I heard if you hammer U.S. coins, they have, like, different metals underneath. We could total get hammered together! Get it!" He laughs at his own joke.

JR looks at me. "Actually, the boys might get along. As long as Luke doesn't have *any* supernatural soccer team preferences."

I shake my head. "It hasn't come up."

"Just check. I don't want a repeat of the Fernando disaster."
(Fernando was a mistake who lasted exactly three dates
during a sad desperate time in my life. The nail in his coffin
was that he liked the Portland Pixies. Danny vetoed him.
Which was fine. Because he slurped his own saliva. He might
have been a blue whale shifter but come on. You gotta
control that shizzle in human form, dude.)

"Yeah, that guy was a tool," Danny's finished his own food
and starts in on JR's.

They start listing Fernando's faults from the singular night
they met him.

I'm starting to go into a food coma and seriously debating
curling up on JR's floor.

But then I get a text. From Luke.

I wanna see you.

And just like that, I'm suddenly awake.

I thank JR and Danny for dinner and head on out.

I call Luke. "Hey, stranger," I smile into the phone, squinting
in the light of the rising sun.

"Hey," I can hear his grin through the phone.

The very sound of his voice sends me into a half-skip down
the sidewalk. I'm so in 'like' with him.

145

"Where are you?" I ask.

"At the hospital."

"WHAT!?" I start running, which is stupid. The hospital is like, miles from JR's. There's no way I'll get there by running. But it's just instinct.

"I started thinking about what you said last morning," Luke replies. "And if you could be part demon … you could be part vamp, you know. Our magic comes from demons. All the dark hearts do, to some degree."

"OMFG!" I stop and hold my phone away from my face to stare at it. Then I hang up and dial Luke on Faceshrine. (Yeah, it's a part-internet-troll knocking off that *other* product, but really, the troll name is more accurate. How much time do you spend looking at the person you're talking to versus yourself? Mirror mirror, anyone?)

Luke picks up and I can see he's in the hospital waiting room, looking fine. No visible burn marks or stakes. I let him have it. "I thought you were hurt!"

His eyebrows shoot up. "Not hurt. I had dinner with a friend in the dermatology department and you came up." My senses go on high alert. Dinner with a friend? What? I mean, we haven't had the exclusivity talk but—my internal rant is distracted, then silenced, then drooling after Luke says, "See, I'm fine," and does a full body scan of himself in a shirt that would make any 1980s romance novel pirate proud. Gah! Why does he have to be so hot?

Luke sees my vapid, pec-obsessed expression when he puts the phone back to his face. He smiles, a bit smug, and says, "George thought to remind me that dark hearts have a natural affinity for one another. So, you might be wrong about that test. It might be accurate."

"I'm still stuck on the name George. I didn't hear anything else you said."

"What. Why?"

"I'm trying to decide whether George is some progressive girl-name or a century-old vamp dude."

Luke smiles and ... dimples. This might be the first time I've totally paid more attention to the face of the other person on the phone during a Faceshrine talk instead of secretly checking my teeth when they aren't looking.

"George is a ... wait for it ... *wonderful* frog shifter."

Jerk! He totally had me thinking he was gonna say woman. "You are a meanie-pooh-head and I'm hanging up—" I reach for the red button.

"Wait!" Luke laughs. "He's a guy. George is a guy. I'm only seeing you, Ly."

I humph. But a smile creeps onto my face despite my best efforts. Damn new relationship highs when I wanna pout and punish Luke for teasing me. I can't! I blow a raspberry at him instead.

"This is the part where you tell me, you're only seeing me," he prompts.

"I'm only seeing you."

"Good. Now come to the hospital and take your silly test. I can't wait to see if you're part vamp." Luke hangs up before I can argue.

I sigh but dial a Broomer. Luke's right. I've put this off long enough.

I meet Luke in the lobby and lead him by memory over to Doctor Eduardo's floor. To my surprise, the part-troll doctor is on duty.

Dr. Eduardo recognizes me immediately and calls out, "Ms. Fox, I didn't expect to see you. One minute."

We stand near the nurse's station and watch a nurse carry a pixie caught in a net. The pixie pouts in the net as the nurse says, "Just one shot and then we'll give you some cotton candy." They round the corner before I can hear the pixie's response. But the idea of cotton candy makes my mouth water.

Eduardo finishes up typing something on the computer and then walks our way.

Luke slips his hand into mine and gives me a reassuring squeeze. (See, isn't he perfect?)

Eduardo runs a hand through his green hair and says, "You ready to take that test?"

"I want cotton candy as a reward."

"That's for children."

I jut out my lip.

Luke asks, "How about for those with a childish attitude?"

Eduardo laughs and leads me over to a chair so I can sit while he stabs me.

We get it over with and I get the world's smallest sugar-substitute disappointment of a cotton candy I've ever seen. It tastes like the grape children's aspirin chewables my dad used to give me. Nose scrunch. I hold the foul fluff in my hand until we're out of Eduardo's line of sight; then I dump it.

"I can't believe they ruined cotton candy. How is that even possible? Doctors are the worst."

Luke laughs and grabs my hand, pulling me to the elevator. "Want a distraction? Want to meet George?"

"Sure," I reply. "Why were you visiting him anyway? Just catching up?"

Luke shakes his head. "I was getting some sun protection spells. You seem to work so late it seemed like the prudent option."

I so wish the elevator was empty right now. I'd jump Luke. But nope. Next to us is a nurse pushing a wheelchair with zombie holding his own severed arm.

So, instead of kissing Luke, I casually ask, "What kind of sun spells did he give you?"

"Couple basic umbrella spells, mirror spells for angled light, some pink cream that's supposed to be a backup layer. All I can say about that one is that I hope it rubs in. I better not turn pink."

"Aww, I'll still date you. Just maybe not in public."

Luke narrows his eyes and yanks on my hand.

"But seriously," I say, as the nurse and her zombie patient exit, "dating me seems too expensive."

He shrugs, "Worth it."

Before I can respond, the door opens onto the dermatology floor and Luke pulls me out of the elevator.

A bug-eyed man with age spots on his face comes forward with a smile. His hand is slightly damp as he shakes mine.

"So, you're Lyon. Great to meet you."

"It's so nice to meet you. Thanks for helping Luke out."

"My pleasure."

"He said you gave him some pink cream. I'm kinda hoping it will dye him like an Easter egg," I toss out.

George laughs. "There's a price for some things, I'm afraid. What I gave him is a blood sweat extract. From hippo shifters. It's how they protect themselves in hippo form. It's initially clear but if it does end up exposed to sunlight, then yes, he will turn a glorious shade of pink."

My eyes light up. "Can I get like ten tubes? There are so many people at work I could use that on." (I briefly imagine switching out all the shampoo in the guy's locker rooms with this stuff. How amazing would it be for all the guys in the office to be walking around with neon pink skin? #newlifegoal)

George grins. "It's prescription only, I'm afraid. Hard to come by."

A nurse comes over to George and says, "Sorry to interrupt, but they're bringing in a sunstroke and burn victim. Found in a field. Guess he's been there a couple days. Disoriented."

"How bad are the burns?"

"Seventy percent."

George sucks in a breath and gives us a look, "Sorry. I better head down to the ER."

We wave as he walks off with the nurse. But George asks one last question before he gets out of earshot, "What kind of victim?"

"Hippo shifter," the nurse answers.

My stomach implodes. The blood drains from my face.

Luke takes a look at me, "Are you alright?"

I shake my head. "I need to call my boss. I just realized something about the case we're working."

I grab my cell and dial Flowers, walking over to an empty exam room. I step inside as Flowers answers.

"Lyon?" he asks.

"Is that Lyon? Tell her I've been waiting for her to visit and give me all the gushy details about Luke!" Sarah's voice pipes up in the background.

"You're at Sarah's?" I'm temporarily distracted.

"Yes. Business discussions. This better be an emergency."

I chew my lip, "I think I might have hurt someone."

"What?" I hear a chair scrape against the floor as Flowers stands. "Just a minute," he tells me. Then he covers the phone with his hand and tells Sarah something, I can't tell what. But I hear him open a door, and then the background is quiet. "Lyon?"

"Yeah?"

"Tell me," he commands.

I take a deep breath, "Um, you know that hippo shifter I lost?"

"Yeah?"

"Well, they're bringing in a hippo shifter to the hospital."

"So?"

"He was found in a field, wandering around. He has severe burns and sunstroke."

"You're at the hospital?"

I nod. Then I realize he can't see me.

"Yup."

"I'll be there in a minute."

I nod again.

Flowers must sense the sick guilt churning in my stomach because he doesn't hang up like I expect. He says, "Lyon, you are allowed to use thorce …" I hear him suppressing a growl, "You can use spells in lithe-threatening situations." The phone drops and I imagine his hand shifted to a tiger paw in his frustration. His voice comes from a distance as he says, "A drug-addled hippo was charging you. You used the minimal magic necessary to protect all o- us and everyone else in that building."

I nod, breathing out. The bile rising in my throat starts to recede. I didn't actually intentionally hurt the hippo. I kept him from hurting other people.

"You did the right thing," Flowers reiterates.

"Right. I did the right thing," I repeat, hoping that saying it aloud will help ease the fear in my stomach. I might have done the right thing, but shit—I hope this shifter isn't hurt. I hope this isn't serious. I should have checked on him. I should have—

Flowers interrupts my thoughts. "Go see where they're putting him. Then text me. I'll meet you there." Flowers hangs up.

I walk out of the exam room and over to Luke. "I'm sorry. This case is open, and my boss wants to—"

Luke leans down and gives me a kiss. "Go do what you do best, Ms. Detective." He reaches into his pocket and pulls out a Peppy Perk Potion. He hands it to me.

"I'm not technically a detective." I unwrap the caffeinated, spelled tablet gratefully.

He grins at me, "You're on your way. Go solve the case. Later, you can come over and solve the mystery of the *rock-hard relic*."

I give a small grin and play along. I bat my eyes and ask, "Will I need my magnifying glass for this relic?"

He narrows his eyes and swats my ass. "Get outta here before I remind you how large that relic is."

I pop the tablet into my mouth, glance at the clock on the wall, and grin. "I might have time for that."

He groans, "Don't tempt me."

I shrug a shoulder, "If I'm part demon, isn't that my job?"

12

I talk with the nurses in the ER, who refuse to give me any information until Flowers shows up and flashes his pretty badge and smile at them.

Then they drop the deets.

Apparently, the hippo's name is Frank Fortinbraugh. I manage not to slap my palm against my forehead, but just barely. I stare at the ceiling for a second and ask, "Why?" as the nurses stare at me. They have no idea how much the letter "f" is starting to haunt me.

I avoid eye contact with Flowers as he continues asking questions of the nurses.

"How'd the patient end up so burnt?"

"Just sun exposure," the nurse shrugs.

But just then, Luke's friend George walks out of a nearby patient room, pulling off blue plastic gloves. He sees me with Flowers and raises his eyebrows. "Lyon?"

"George, this is my boss. Officer Diego Flores," I gesture at Flowers.

The two men shake hands.

I explain why we're stalking the good doctor. "I couldn't help overhearing your nurse as you walked away, sir, and I think we may need to speak with your patient."

George's eyebrows lift. "Is it something that can wait? He's in rough shape. We had to put him on a couple heavy animal tranquilizers. His hippo was pretty reluctant to shift."

Flowers shakes his head. "I wish we could wait, but he's wanted for questioning in connection with an open case. Can you tell me exactly what happened to him?"

George shakes his head sadly. "I've seen it once or twice before. Someone drained his blood sweat. So, when the sun rose, he had no protection."

I pipe up, "Blood sweat? Isn't that the stuff you gave Luke?"

George nods. "Yup. Some hippo shifters donate it and wizard labs spell it to enhance it. But Frank doesn't remember donating. I asked. Stuff goes for a pretty penny, so some hippos give more than they should. There's a decent black market for it with the vamps."

I make eye contact with Flowers and then ask the doc, "But, I thought blood sweat was pink."

"It only turns pink when it's exposed to sunlight. Before that, it's just clear, kind of like sweat."

"Or maybe like urine?" I ask.

George makes a disgusted face. "I suppose."

"Those jars?" I turn to Flowers and raise my eyebrows. "At the shack?"

Flowers nods his head and tells me, "Lyon, call the lab. Ask them about … see… did they test those jars? Maybe they weren't urine. I'll start questioning … the patient." Flowers gets visibly more upset each time he realizes he has to rephrase to avoid the 'forbidden' letter.

George reaches out and holds onto Flowers' arm. "You should probably know, he still had trace amounts of Nappies in his system when he came in. He's slipped back into baby talk a couple times. That can happen with long-term addicts. I'm not sure how good he'll do with the questioning."

Their voices fade as I walk down the hall to make the call to the ME's office.

Zoe answers the phone herself and tells me that they don't even have the urine jars at the lab. Apparently, the BM lab specializes in handling hazardous waste. At my snicker, Zoe clarified, "That's the Bio-Magical Lab, Lyon. Not the bowel movement lab, come on."

"Oh please, you know you snicker about it, too," I said. "Because they basically handle shit."

"Well, their director, Fabian Dark, *is* a total prick."

"Then he'll be a total expert for our urine jars. You know because he's a…" My cursing curse won't let me say prick, "penis-face." I face palm it. "Never mind."

"I thought you were looking for blood sweat," Zoe doesn't even fake laugh at my stupid joke and then points out my logical inconsistencies. If we were face to face, I'd want to blow a raspberry at her. People like that are the worst! Too mature to be any fun. Ugh. I don't know what Bennett sees in her. (Don't say legs. I'll punch you.)

"Well I gotta get going, my boss just got here," I hang up the phone before Zoe can say anything else.

I look up the BM lab, call, and get told we have to go down there in person and flash our badges in order to get test results. The automated message tells me they've had too many prank callers trying to vocally hypnotize staff into stealing samples to allow any over-the-phone discussions. Who would want to steal samples of troll sweat or were-bear hair? Blech.

I come out of the room to find George just walking off and Flowers still in the hall. "Dead-end," I tell him. "We'll have to go in person to the lab after this."

"Correction," Flowers replies, "you'll have to go. I have another interview with a matchmaking client."

I furrow my brows. "In the morning?"

Flowers heads down the hall without answering me. Frankly, I'm shocked he even told me he had a matchmaking 'interview' aka date he's unaware he's having. Flowers is usually super tight-lipped about anything in his personal life. Maybe Sarah and Tabby are right about dating loosening him up.

Flowers strolls into Frank's hospital room as if he owns the place.

Frank Fortinbraugh lays in a large tub full of sparkling green liquid goop. Two tubes are attached to one of his arms and a glowing blue orb flies slowly up and down his body. He's skinny as a rail, like most serious addicts are. I can't remember much about his hippo form other than the giant teeth, but this guy is emaciated, and I wonder if his hippo is, too. Frank's got greasy black hair and heavy eyelids with long straight lashes. His brown eyes slide back and forth between Flowers and me.

Flowers jerks his head at the patient, indicating I should introduce us.

We get through the formalities, flash the badges, and get down to questions.

"So Frank, how often did you go see Louise?" I ask.

Frank sighs and scratches at one of the IVs in his arm. "I'm not sure, really. Couple times a month? He was always trying to convince me to go *ga-ga-goo...*" he shakes his head to snap out of the baby talk. "Sorry 'bout that. I've got a stutter."

Yeah, stutter my ass. This guy takes Nappies way more than a couple times a month.

Flowers isn't thrown off at all by the baby talk. He's probably seen it before. "Who tried to get you to go?"

"Hopper. I always thought that dude was just chasing a good time, but," Frank narrows his eyes, "now I wonder... was he just using me? Did he do this to me? Drain and dump? When I get outta here we are going to have words."

I suppress the guilt that stabs my stomach. Frank is blaming his friend for dumping him. Technically, that part was my fault. Of course, I didn't know he'd been drained of blood sweat at the time. Otherwise, I could have wished him into an abandoned vamp lair or hippo zoo exhibit or something.

I take a deep breath before asking, "Have you felt like this before? Gotten sunburnt like this before after using?"

The little blue orb buzzes around Frank's face and he waves it away. "Honestly, I don't remember."

"Did you always go to Louise's nap shack?"

"Yeah. Hopper always insisted on her." He shakes his head. "Now, I know why. She let him do this. She always was a bitch—*poo-poo head*—anyway. Never wanted to let me use the tub to nap out. *That meanie old lady!*" His tone rises a couple octaves and his bottom lip starts to tremble.

Flowers sighs and just presses the button for the nurse.

Frank lets out a wail. *"My fwiend was mean to me!"*

A nurse pops her head in, and Flowers says calmly, "I think we're gonna need a bottle in here."

She gives a brief nod and pops back out.

As I watch Frank throw a toddler-like fit in the tub, I think back to his hippo form, the couple seconds I saw it. He probably would have broken the tub at her place as the Nappies wore off.

"Sounds like Louise was kind of mean to you, too." I say, trying to get on his good side. But really, can you get on a toddler's good side?

We have to wait until the nurse brings in a baby bottle of milk and Frank takes a few pulls before he can talk again.

"She was. She really was mean—*I no like Louise*. I mean, the customer is always right, you know? Not Louise. Nope. I swear, she took that job because she liked bossing people around. *She's not the boss of me. I sit on her. Smash her up.*"

He seems like he has some violent tendencies. Hates Louise. Or is that just the unrestrained baby-talk? I'm not sure but I feel like Frank's too fried to do something subtle, like hex a knife. That's too understated, almost catty. I mean the hex on the knife means Louise technically killed herself. That takes brain power. This dude clearly doesn't have it.

I tilt my head. "How do you know she didn't drain you herself?"

Frank's nostrils flare. "She did this to me? Louise?" He shoves the bottle back in his mouth and starts rapidly sucking.

Flowers steps up, elbowing me in the side as he does. Crap. I shouldn't have said that. I was just thinking—a woman who doesn't mind hiding overdosed dragon bodies and collecting pee for crazy unknown reasons might not bat an eye at collecting blood sweat. For all I know, all those jars could be blood sweat. Part of me is itching to go to BM and find out.

Flowers tried to calm Frank down, "We don't know that. She's just guessing. It could be Hopper. Why do you think it was him?"

"Hopper's always looking for his next big win. Always trying to get one over on somebody. *He's so smarty pants.*" Frank winces as the blue healing orb focuses on a rough-looking burn on his hand. *"Owie!"*

"What's Hopper's real name?"

"Francis Dogle. But he won't answer if you call him that. Hates his name."

"Thank goodness," I mutter. Why the hell does every male on this case have to have a damned letter 'f' in his name? "Where's he work?"

"He doesn't. Usually just hangs 'round his house."

"If he doesn't work, how does he afford a house?" (Wish I could do that.)

"Girlfriend's house. He usually goes through a couple a year once they figure out he's not just down on his luck but a lazy-ass leech," Frank says.

"Why d'you like him?" Shit. That wasn't a good cop kind of question. But I can't help myself.

"He's funny."

"You always get high together?"

"Nah." After a beat, he said, "Yeah."

"You happen to have his current address?"

Frank gestures toward his phone, which is charging on the nightstand. "You all going to charge him for this? I think he needs—*timeout!!! You put him in a timeout!*" Frank shakes his head trying to shake off the baby talk. But he winces, then hisses, as if the movement makes something hurt.

Flowers nods, "We'll check into it. We see enough evidence to prove he took your blood sweat, then we'll charge him."

"Good." Frank shoves his thumb into his mouth and starts sucking. His eyelids start to droop.

Flowers gently pries the bottle out of Frank's hand as Frank drifts off. I watch in admiration/confusion. It's almost like Flowers has done this kind of thing before. He was really patient with the whole baby talk thing. Which is not normal for Flowers. I start to wonder who he knew that was addicted to Nappies. But I don't ask. I know better.

I go to Frank's phone, grab the number and the address for Hopper and follow Flowers into the hall.

"Thoughts?" I ask.

Flowers waits until we're alone on the elevator before he says, "Maybe Louise and Hopper were consistently draining -rank. Maybe they were partners. Maybe Hopper didn't want to split the gold anymore. Maybe he killed Louise so he could sell the blood sweat himsel-."

It's a good theory.

"You think that's more likely than Freddie wanting to inherit the nap shack?"

Flowers shrugs. "We don't have evidence o- either yet. I don't think either one is smart enouth—Dammit! Even enouth?" Flowers grinds his lips together and takes a moment before he continues, "smart to hire out a hex. Definitely not to complete a hex themselves on this case."

"Yeah, hexes are complicated … right?" I have no idea. I've never looked into them.

"Yup. There's almost a science to them. They're magical writing that's kinda like an equation. Have to have all the little bits just right. Right order or it'll blow up in your … ass."

I decide to move onto another question that's been nagging me.

"Any news on the dragon?"

Flowers sighs and says, "William Henson. Age twenty-two. Originally -rom Wisconsin. He was a rogue."

My heart drops. "Fluck." Bennett's not gonna take that well. There's no one out there to avenge William's death. No one to take care of burial. "Commander French know?"

Flowers looks over at me and raises an eyebrow.

"What?" I ask defensively. "It's gotta hit close to home, right? I'm just … concerned."

Flowers chews on his lip instead of answering me. The silence and his judgment grow really uncomfortable. "Not yet. I know it's gonna hit him hard."

I nod.

We get to the bottom floor and Flowers grins. "Enjoy your visit to the lab. I'm about to go to Wanda's Brews to interview a smoking hot twenty-six-year-old."

I narrow my eyes and flip him the bird.

As he strolls off, I group text Seena and Becca.

Emergency spymasters needed. Flowers is about to go on date 2. Who can film it?

My phone pings the second I've sent the text.

Becca's response is two words. *Hell yes!*

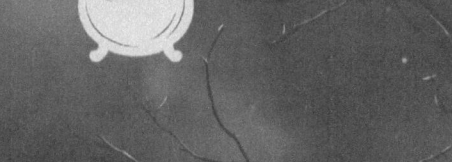

13

The lab is as shiny as a newly-scrubbed toilet. White and gleaming.

I flash my badge and get magically scanned by a wizard. When he's satisfied that I'm not there to steal any of their "shit" he lets me in. A squeaky-voiced little dude with buck teeth leads me to his office, which is just a sterile and boring as everything else, except for a Deadpool bobblehead. He types into the computer while clicking his tongue against his teeth and confirms that some of the jars from the nap shack were blood sweat.

"Some? What you mean some?"

Squeaky bites his lower lip, a bad habit for a guy with buck teeth. "Only nine jars were blood sweat."

"Nine jars out of how many?"

"Twenty-seven."

I furrow my brow. "What the heck was in the rest of the jars then?"

Squeaky's breath hisses out between his teeth. (I'm temporarily super-glad I do not work with Squeaky. Like everything about him is annoying.) "Shifter pee. I thought you all already knew that."

I refrain from sticking my tongue out at Squeaky. But just barely. I'm tired, I'm hungry, I want to go home. Actually, I want to go spy on Flowers then go home. But I know my furry-butt boss is gonna give me a hard time if I don't come back with a zillion details. So, I ask, "Any particular kind of shifter pee?"

He clicks through a few screens and his brow furrows. He clicks again and says, "Interesting."

(See—annoying. He's saying something and nothing at once.)

I ignore personal space and walk around his desk to peer over his shoulder, "What's interesting?"

"It looks like all the pee comes from mixed breed shifters."

"What do you mean? What's so special about mixed shifter pee?" (My life is so strange. I'm having a serious conversation about urine with a stranger.)

"It's not what's special. It's ... mixed magic does weird things. Depending on the two types of shifters, the magic can interact oddly."

I circle my hand in the universal 'keep going' gesture.

Squeaky clicks through a couple more screens and stops on one. "See here, chicken-dogs?"

"Chickie pups," I correct him. Chickie pups sounds way better.

Squeaky points at the screen. "See the magic levels?" He points to a chart with a jagged line that goes up and down like some heart monitor line.

"Yup. What about it?" I have no idea what magic is supposed to look like on a chart.

"The two magics are fighting each other."

"But ... why?" I ask, even though this conversation is starting to resemble the conversation I had with Bennett earlier. What had he said? Thank God he wasn't a dragon deer?

Squeaky shrugs and says, "Why the magic fights is heavily debated. No one knows for sure why. I side with predator-prey theorists that basic instinct causes the magic to be at odds. Honestly, I think it causes some mental instability, too. Had a cousin who was an eagle mouse. It was kind of like he had split-personalities or something. I'm telling you ... odd. The magic levels in the urine are volatile."

I squint at the screen. I get that Louise was collecting blood sweat for cash. She could get good money for that. But what about pee? Who would want crazy shifter pee? Why collect it? It doesn't make sense.

"Can you print out the info for every jar for me? Including the shifter combos for all the urine samples, please?"

Squeaky does and I ask more about mixed shifter theories. Because, suddenly, I'm wondering if all this applies to me. I mean fae sweet heart and demon dark heart magic? Those are pretty opposite, right? I am a little eccentric ... not crazy. (Don't even.) But, like, is my chicken leg some kind of weird reaction? Like my magic is fighting inside? Is that why I didn't know I had any magic forever? My magic fought itself?

I have a moment in the middle of the BM Lab.

My magic fighting itself would explain a lot. Suddenly, I'm somewhat eager to find out the results of the lab test.

I turn to Squeaky, who's been answering my question with long-winded, science-y words. And I bite my lip and say, "I don't understand any of that." (It's better than saying I wasn't listening.)

Squeaky sighs and dumbs it down for me. "Other people theorize that the opposite magics have a nullifying effect on each other, decreasing or washing out the power. That simple enough?"

I nod and take the sheets of paper he hands me. That would definitely explain my current theory about my own magic.

"Anything else?" he asks me.

"Just one question. Fae blood work the same?"

Squeaky laughs. "You think we get a lotta that in here? Those fae kings quash everything they can. Want all the control beyond the Veil." He shakes his head. "Inconclusive. We haven't been able to do enough studies to show they're the same."

That stinks. So, I still have no idea how my magic operates. "Got it," I tell Squeaky as I shuffle through the papers, looking at the urine samples Louise-the-weirdo-drug-dealing-blood-sweat-and-urine-collecting … her insulting name needs work. Louise the asshole. Except I'll never be able to say that out loud. Louise the doo-doo head. That seems childishly appropriate for a Nappie dealer. Louise the doo-doo head it is.

There's urine from the squirrel-rhino, the chickie pups, some animal labeled a cat peacock … that must be frickin' gorgeous. I'm distracted briefly as I wonder if that would be like a black peacock with a cat head or like a cat with feathers and a peacock tail. Damn. I wish that shifter had been there when we busted the nap shack so I could tell.

I shuffle through the pages, but no lizard bear pee is in the pile. So Lilypunt's pee wasn't collected. I don't see the grasshorse either. I wonder if their animal forms are too small to get samples from. I mean, I woulda' thought the chickie pups would be too small too, but with the dog in them, who knows? Maybe they lift a claw and spray?

I feel a desperate need to stop what I'm doing and call JR. Or maybe Luke. I need to tell someone about the fact that I'm trying to imagine mixed animal shifters peeing. That's just one of those traumatic moments that has to be shared, you know?

Since, technically, JR works in law enforcement and this is an open case, I pick her.

I text: *I'm currently trying to imagine how a chickie pup pees. Just sharing so you get the awesome mental image stuck in your head, too.*

She responds, *Maybe they fly and spray. Like a crop duster.*

I bust up laughing and Squeaky gives me a weird look. But this is why she's in the inner circle. JR just rolls with my weirdness.

I totally can picture a chickie pup barking as it flies low and sprays the grass, thinking, 'That's right mutha' fuckers. This is my yard!'

I thank Squeaky and leave. I Broomer over to Wanda's Brews, a nice little pub JR and I like to hit up for happy hour sometimes. When I land, I text Becca.

I'm here. Is Flowers still on his date?

Becca replies, *Oh yes. And you're gonna want to see this. Seena
and I have a booth in the back left corner.*

My curiosity peaked; I head into Wanda's. It's got some
televisions blaring sports on one side of the bar and then a
bunch of booths on the other. It takes a second for my eyes
to adjust to the mood lighting, but once they do, I spot
Flowers and his date right away. I have to bite down on a
grin as I see a pained look on his face. I crane my neck to see
his date. Sitting across from him in an outfit that would
make any hooker proud, is a full-fledged demon. Black horns
protrude from her forehead, she has those way over-penciled
thick eyebrows, beautiful long lashes, black hair, and deep
orange eyes. Her skin is smooth and silky, and her large
breasts spill out of the tiny leather bra she wears. It doesn't
help that she has her elbows on the table pushing up her
cleavage even more. I watch Flowers struggle to maintain
eye contact. It is hilarious.

I walk back to Seena and Becca's table. Flowers does not
notice me at all (for obvious reasons.) Becca shamelessly has
her phone out and pointed at Flowers, recording his entire
miserable experience.

I slide into the booth and nod at the golem bartender who
nods back at me, his clay hands looking slightly muddy after
all the drinks he's mixed. (The place is packed because
Wanda's has amazing garlic fries.)

"So, what's happened?" I ask, as I steal a bite of Becca's quadruple sugar cream pie. It's got molasses, honey, white fae-suckle flowers, and brown sugar all mixed in at the bottom and then this creamy meringue thing going on. It's heaven.

Seena snorts and pushes his glasses up his nose. "What hasn't happened is a better question."

"What do you mean?"

Seena pushes around some carrots left on his plate, "First thing she asked when she sat was, 'Favorite sex position?' Flowers about fell out of his seat."

My jaw drops. I stare wide-eyed at Becca, looking for confirmation that Seena's not pulling my leg. She nods.

"Tell me you got that on video," I beg.

Becca shakes her head sadly. "I had no idea she was gonna go there. I pulled out the camera right after, so you won't miss too much."

I grab her arm. "Details. His face? What did it look like when she asked that?"

Seena throws his head back and laughs. "Oh, man! Remember when you bonked him in the head with that yoga block?"

I nod.

"That face. That shocked, 'hell no that didn't just happen' face."

I picture that face in all its glory, directed at someone else. (I don't mention how often I've seen that face from Flowers.)

Becca pipes up, "He immediately started lecturing her. Telling her that wasn't appropriate first date conversation."

I press my lips together and stare over at sexy demon girl. "I imagine she didn't take that well?"

"Oh, she just smiled and got her phone out. We couldn't tell from here, but from Flower's face, I'm pretty sure she started showing him nudies."

"The words 'sexual compatibility is important' might have drifted over," Seena says.

"More like, we were so nosy that I sent Seena on a trip to the bathroom and he detoured by their table," Becca adds.

I can't hold it in. I bust a gut. I mean, really? "What are Sarah and Tabby thinking? Flowers is probably the most uptight person I know!"

Seena nods. "I'm shocked he hasn't left yet."

"He can't, he thinks this is a job," Becca points out as she zooms a little more on her camera phone. "Thanks for asking us to do this, BTW. Totes awesome night."

I watch as the demon woman stands and makes her way to the women's restroom.

I can't resist. I stand and follow, telling Becca and Seena, "I'll be back," with a wink.

When I'm washing my hands, the demon woman comes up beside me. And obviously, I'm not the best at keeping my mouth shut. I say, "Hey, you don't know me. I'm Lyon. You're on a date with my boss. I just wanted to let you know—"

"You're Lyon?" The demon woman's eyes widen, the orange color of her irises sparking a bit red around the edges. (I've never met a full demon before, so I have no idea if that's normal.) She holds out her hand. "Pleasure to meet you."

Oh crap. "Did Flowers talk about me?" Dammit all.

"Flowers? You mean Flores? Diego Flores?"

"Yeah, sorry. That's his office nickname."

The demon woman smiles and says, "Nope. I heard about you from Sarah and Tabby. They play a lot of bingo with my grandmother."

"Oh," Relief rushes through me and I extend my hand to shake. It warms slightly on contact with hers.

Demon woman's eyes widen as we shake. "They told me your boss liked to give you a hard time. So, they asked if I could give him one."

My heart twists up a bit. "They did?" That's probably the most evil/thoughtful/perfect thing anyone's ever done for me. Not gonna lie, my eyes mist a bit as I think of my neighbor and her best friend. They really are amazing.

"Yup," Demon woman smiles. "I'm happy to help. I'm Nicolette, by the way."

"Well, Nicolette, it sounds like you're doing amazing. I'm super grateful." I give her a wide smile and Nicolette's eyes flash red again, this time stronger.

"So, Sarah and Tabby didn't tell me you were part-demon," she leans against the counter. "No wonder you and your boss don't get along. He's about as strait-laced as it gets."

I arch a brow. "Wait. You can tell I'm part demon?"

Nicolette gives me a weird look. "Yeah. All demons can recognize each other. At least a little. We're drawn to each other."

"Hmm, I didn't know that." I mean, Luke kinda said that. But I didn't really believe it. I've always just thought vamps were hot AF. I shake my head. "I'm sorry. Raised human. I know basically nothing about being a demon. I didn't even know I might be part-demon until like a week ago."

Nicolette bites her lip. "Well, normally, I'd say good luck and leave it at that. But since Tres has lots of part-demons, and you're friends with Tabby and Sarah, I'm gonna warn you— you kinda need to know the hierarchy."

"There's a hierarchy?"

"Oh, yeah," her face is super-serious. "Lower-ranking demons cannot mess with higher-ranked ones. It's, like, genetically programmed into us. If you try, there are serious consequences."

I lean against the counter next to Nicolette. I have to lean to the side slightly because her black horns are at eye level and those suckers are pointy. "So, do you mind? Totally ignorant here. I spent most of my life thinking I was only part-fae. What the heck is the hierarchy?"

"Well, short version: it's all organized by the 'supposed' deadly sins. Lowest level are the lazies. So, sloth demons, who literally are like those losers who go around and tempt people into marathon video game sessions. Typically, they stick to the human-only cities since they're lowest on the totem pole. They get picked on and can't really retaliate ... because, you know, hellish consequences if you violate the hierarchy."

"Punny."

She winks. "I've been known to toss out a good one now and then."

"Wow. Makes sense. I hope that's not what I am," I say, but I don't hold out much hope. I chew my lip as I wonder. I mean, I am lazy. I love reading and laying on the couch. Hate cooking and cleaning. Have like zero cool powers or glowing eyes. I sigh. I probably am a damn sloth demon. Crapola. Of course. "With my luck, that's exactly what I am."

"What do you mean?"

"Blood and magic test—waiting for results," I explain. "I don't even know if that blood and magic test will identify the type of demon I am. Or just that I am part-demon."

Nicolette shrugs. "Never done one. My mom's the part-demon in my fam. I can't tell what you are, just when we shook hands that you have some demon in you. But, anyway, the other types are anger or wrath ... those demons made the vamps with their bloodlust. Then gluttony demons are above that. I'm part envy-demon, we're the fourth most powerful. The only demons higher than us are lust, greed, then pride demons."

I shake my head. "I totally need to get over to Tall Tales and buy a book on this." I sigh. "After I figure out how to reverse engineer my other powers."

Nicolette scrunches her face. "Why would anyone want to reverse their powers?"

I cough uncomfortably. "I kinda made Flowers lose the letter 'f' from his vocab. Now he can't say any word with that letter at all."

Nicolette laughs—her laugh is totally scary movie villain worthy—startling a wererabbit, who ducks under the bathroom stall door and hops out of the restroom's animal flap without even washing her hands.

"That is the best!" Nicolette says, clapping her hands. "I better get back out there. He probably wonders if I dined and ditched him."

I smile, "He's probably hoping for it."

She raises her eyebrows and gives me a silly grin. "Oh no. He's got more fun coming to him. And now, I'm gonna try and trap him into saying 'eff words' all night."

She raises her hand and gives me a high five before she leaves the bathroom.

I fluff my hair in the mirror and stare at myself for a minute. If that's what demons are like, it might not be so bad to be one. Even if I'm just a slothy one.

Then I skip on out, eager to watch the rest of Flower's torture session.

14

Nicolette drags out Flowers' personal hell for another half an hour. My ribs hurt from laughing so hard.

But Flowers catches me on his way out. "Lyon!" he barks.

I jump in my seat, staring with wide eyes at Seena and Becca.

"You are supposed to be researching reversals," Flowers growls, leaning over me and into the booth. His fingers clench the booth material so hard that I'm pretty sure he's fighting against his claws popping out in public.

Dammit. Nicolette left him in an awful mood.

"Just grabbing a bite and was about to get to it, sir," I tack on the 'sir' in the hope that it'll buy me a little leniency.

Flowers closes his eyes and does a calming breath. "Be early, tomorrow night. I want a report on your progress."

I nod. Fuck. It's gonna be another long morning for Lyon sponsored by the makers of Peppy Perk.

I've left my spell reversal books in my locker. So, I sigh and start to walk from Wanda's back to the office. I snatch out a book or two, before Luke texts.

Where you at?

Leaving works. You?

Picking you up.

I smile. I type, *You aren't sick of me yet?*

I walk down the stairs and out the door, waiting for Luke's reply text. I don't get one. Instead I feel a rush of wind as Luke uses his supernatural speed to run up and snatch me off my feet.

"My place or yours?" he asks.

I rearrange myself so my books are in one hand and I can wrap one arm around his massive shoulders and stroke his shoulder length blond hair.

"Mine." The word isn't even all the way out of my mouth before he races along the sidewalk, carrying me past lumbering trolls and drunk witches. Just as my mouth starts to get dry from the wind constantly whipping at my lips, we arrive.

Of course, Sarah and Tabby spill out of Sarah's apartment the moment they see us.

"Well aren't you just grinnin' like a possum eating a tater," Sarah says when she sees Luke.

That just makes him grin wider. "Yes ma'am."

I jump out of Luke's arms and give Sarah Snow and Tabby hugs. "Thank you both so much. Flowers' date this morning was hilariousness incarnate."

"Of course, sugar," Sarah says as she pats my back.

Tabby shakes her head. "That man has such a stick up his ass that I'm surprised he can shit."

Sarah waves her hand, "I don't think he can. That poor boy's so backed up his eyes are brown."

I facepalm it on that one. I totally agree that Flowers is uptight. But I don't want to be thinking about his tiger butt at all. "Too visual. Too visual," I scold them.

Tabby rolls her eyes. "How can you work murder cases if you can't stand a silly little discussion like this?"

I shrug.

Tabby shakes her head and grabbed Sarah's arm. "Well, we'd better get back to it. We're getting one of those phone games built. And then a couple of my cat shifter friends are coming over for a game of feathers."

"Phone games?" I ask.

"Apps," Sarah corrects Tabby. "I keep telling her, they're called apps. Our matchmaking business is getting an app."

Tabby sniffs dismissively. "App isn't even a real word."

"Yes it is—" Sarah starts to argue. You can tell by the tired tone of her voice that they've had this argument a million times already.

Luke interrupts with a question, "What are you naming the app?"

Tabby says, "I wanted to go with blue snow match me. I mean we need to make people familiar with our brand."

Sarah crosses her arms and taps her high-heeled foot. "And I said that that is way too long for a phone. People don't want to have to scroll down to read the name of your business. I suggested mate maker."

"But that's totally shifter biased!" Tabby exclaims. "Trust me, I am all about the hot shifters … but our business needs to be for all supernaturals."

"What about initials?" I suggest. And I roll my eyes and say, "Never mind," when I realize their initials will spell BS Matchmaking. That might be an accurate name, but not good marketing.

"Don't you worry about us, sweetie, we'll figure it out. You and Luke go have a nice morning, now. You should be getting that boy inside before it gets any brighter out here," Sarah gestures at the sunrise starting to peek over the treetops across the road.

I nod. "Good luck, ladies. And thanks again for the Flowers thing."

Sarah nods. Tabby winks. Then they link elbows and stroll back toward Sarah's apartment, already bickering about app names again. "—No. I'm vetoing Your Other Half. Do you know how many Frankenstein creatures that will pull in? They're all looking for better hands, bigger feet. What if they confuse us with that body part auction house? Hand Jobs or whatever it's called—insurance alone for that ..." Tabby's voice trails off as the door shuts.

"Knowing them must make life very ... exciting," Luke says diplomatically.

I pop my lips. "Understatement."

Luke and I get settled into my purple velvet couch and open up the books that Flowers sent me. Luke's the sweetest. He's agreed to help me skim the books so I can figure out how to reverse my ability to lose things.

I yawn. "Sucks that I have to be back at work in six hours." I shoot up in my seat. "Shoot!"

"What?" Luke looks over at me as he pops open a button on his collar.

"I have to go get my uniform. I forgot it at the dry cleaners. And I'm pretty sure they have a pickup time limit before they donate to some charity—like The Shift-nation Army."

Luke scrunches his nose. "You took your uniform to a dry cleaner?"

I glance at the clock and grab my keys. "Yup. Got puke on it at a crime scene—" I wink at Luke. "I'll be right back. Don't go through my panty drawer."

"Now, you know if you say something like that …"

I smile as I pull my purse over my shoulder, "I know. Have fun."

I chuckle as I walk down the stairs and the few blocks to Sue's Cleaners. The bell dings as I walk in to find a very familiar wizard lined up in front of the counter with his droopy hat at his side. I roll my eyes and stare at the wall as he gets helped by the same punk rock girl that I saw last time. Marian—the all-in-black look is accented by chains and a collar today. I watch as she argues with the wizard. It's like deja vu. Only this time, I don't intervene. She gives the wizard a lot of 'tude.

I pretend not to hear them argue as I stare at a cork board with all kinds of announcements on it: roommate wanted fliers, spell caster ads, missed magical connections, and missing people. In the bottom corner, near a flier for an exotic snake dancer, are two missing person papers. They look homemade. Definitely not from my office. One shows a witch with wild red hair named Rachel. On her neck is a tattoo with the letters EWNM. Next to her is some boy-next-door type with blond hair whose pic says he goes by Bill. The girl's tattoo makes me think about our interview. Lilypunt said he saw a girl with orange or pink hair. What if it was red? She had a neck tattoo right? Initials? Four letters is too much for initials. But my intuition sparks.

I grab the flier and stare at it while the wizard in front of me stomps off in a huff. Apparently, he won't be getting a stiff 'hat' today.

I step to the front of the line. "Pick up for Lyon Fox."

Marian eyes me dully, pops her gum and stares boredly at the computer until she finds me in the system. Then her eyes widen. She turns from the screen to me and clears her throat. "Oh, yeah. Um … about your uniform. That baby who spit up on you was a zombie."

I crinkle my brows. "Okaay…" He didn't look like a zombie. But then, if Nappies revert people to their baby state, maybe zombies turn back into human babies? I don't really know. I add that to the list of endless annoying questions I need ask Seena instead of looking things up on a search engine like Wing or Goblin. Because, for some reason, talking into the little computer mic is way harder than bugging my desk-buddy. I glance back at Marian, who's waving her heavily ringed hands and still talking.

"So, whoever spit up on you is a zombie baby who like, must have crawled through radioactive waste or something. We don't have a product to counteract radioactivity."

"No spell?"

She shakes her head. "Sorry. Your uniform was toast. I thought Sue called you about it."

I bite down on the pit that opens up in my stomach at that news. Thanks to the key lime pie I bought while I watched Flowers physically shake under the weight of Nicolette's demonic stare, I do not currently have enough gold to buy a new uniform in my account. "Tiger claws!" I mutter. I hate my life.

Marian looks concerned. "Dude, it's just a uniform. You okay?"

I shake it off because there's nothing else I can do but stew. I've got a hot guy at my apartment. I've got more important things to do.

I turn to leave but Marian stops me. "Hey! You can't take that flier."

I look down at Rachel's flier. "Why not?"

"I ... we don't have any more. And in case someone's seen her..."

I tilt my head. "You know this Rachel girl?"

Marian bites her black lips. "Did. Before she bolted."

"She a shifter?" I ask.

Marian licks her lips and her tongue turns a nasty sickly shade of grey from her black lipstick. "Maybe."

"What do you mean, maybe?"

Marian narrows her eyes at me. "I mean what-the-hell business is it of yours?"

I roll my eyes and toss the flier on the counter. I take a picture with my phone. "Just think I might know someone who might have seen her."

"What?" Marian's hands go flat on the counter. Her eyes are wide and shocked. Then her voice gets small and vulnerable. "I've tried calling. Going by her place. No one answers. At first I thought she might be avoiding me ..." She shakes off the sadness and gets gruff again. "Take it then, if you know someone who's seen her. Just ... if you find anything out, will you let me know?"

I look down at Marian, who's clearly struggling to hold it together. Her tattoo-sleeved arms come up and she wraps them around herself. She looks lost in that moment.

The fight drains out of me and I grab Rachel's flier. Then I go scoop up the one for the guy, too. "I'm gonna take both. I'll tell my boss. Police will keep an eye peeled for them, alright?"

Marian nods, her face pale.

Poor kid. I don't want to say anything, but if her friend Rachel was mixed up at the nap shack, things don't look good. At least not from where I'm standing.

I leave and tuck the missing fliers into my purse. I walk home wishing that the world were a different place.

Coming home to find my apartment smells like a chocolate factory makes my jaw drop. I find Luke in the kitchen, wearing only an apron, and pulling homemade brownies out of my oven.

"What is going on here?" I ask with a smile.

Luke looks a little startled. "That was quick." He glances at my hands. "I thought you were picking up your uniform."

"Apparently, it was ruined."

Luke takes off my chicken-shaped oven mitt and comes and gives me a nearly naked hug. "Sorry. But I'm kinda glad. They use all kinds of nasty chemicals, spells, shifter—"

I've literally resisted as long as fairly possible. But I smack his butt and interrupt his sentence. I mean it was just there!

I laugh. "So, is naked cooking something I need to be aware of?"

He shrugs, "I was just trying to surprise you. I picked up some instant-brownie mix from Cherry last time I saw her. Thought it would be a fun little thing to tempt you with."

"You can tempt me with brownies any day."

He goes back to the oven and cuts a tiny brownie out for me. He blows on it and pops it into my mouth.

Then we share a chocolate-coated kiss.

15

Half an hour later, Luke's dressed, our appetites are sated (by brownies duh, what were you thinking? ;)), and he and I flip through the books on spell reversal. I try to keep my eyelids peeled open, but they're drooping.

"Okay! I think I got it!" Luke looks up excitedly. When he sees me practically asleep, leaning on my hand, he shoves me.

My head falls off my hand and nearly smacks the table. Only his vamp speed saves me. His cold hand swoops underneath my face and cradles my cheek just before I hit.

I blink a few times. "Nothing like violence to wake a girl up." I push myself off the dining table and lean back in my chair.

"Violence, please!" Luke rolls his eyes. He stands up, practically bouncing on his feet. "Come on! I think I might have a solution. Up! Up!"

I stretch and begrudgingly stand. I crack my neck as I ask, "Okay, what do I do?"

"Well, first, we need to make me lose something, like Flowers, so we can test this."

"I'm not taking away a letter."

"Come on. X is not a very important letter. Take that one."

"Happens to be at the end of my favorite word, which starts with S-E—"

"Fine," Luke laughs. "Not a letter. How about a number? Like a really high number? 4,872?"

"What if that makes you lose all those numbers? You need measurements at work. How are you gonna build a three-quarter inch caster if you lose the number four? You can't operate without half the numbers."

He sighs and runs a hand through his gorgeous, shoulder-length blond hair. "A phrase then? Skinna marinky dinky dink, skinna marinky doo—" he starts to sing.

"How about zigazig ah?" I ask.

He laughs. "I know that song. Isn't it Nice Ghouls?"

"Spice Ghouls."

"Not a fan?"

I wave a hand. "No. Totally a fan. I've just been trying to force JR into a duet for years and if you couldn't finish the line, I'd totally take you to karaoke and make you sing with me."

"But that's the part of the song that gets all the glory."

My grin widens. "I know."

Luke just grins, shaking his head. "As you wish."

"That's right, DPR."

Luke raises his brows.

"You're my Dead Pirate Roberts."

"Clever. Alright then, lose my zigazig ah. Let's test this baby."

"You sure?"

"Yup."

I clear my throat and stare into his brilliant blue eyes. "You've lost your zigazig ah."

Luke poses and lifts his heels up and down rapidly and he tosses his arms out, side to side. He shakes his hips as good as any drag queen I've ever seen. And he starts singing Spice Ghouls. He knows all the words, which just makes me cup my hands over my mouth to smother my laughter. "If you want the power to hover, let me eat your friends. They won't last forever, but ghoulship never ends. I wanna huh, I wanna huh, I wanna huh …. And I really really really wanna—"

"Zigazig ah!" I jump up and finish the song like we're onstage, standing in front of him and stealing all the applause.

Luke grins and turns me around before my jazz hands get too tired. "Alright. That worked. Now, to test out reversal." Luke grabs the book he was looking at and hands it to me. Then he goes into my kitchen and grabs a sharpie.

"Look at you, all making yourself at home with my sharpies and my aprons."

He bites his lip and I can see a bit of fang. "I hope that's okay."

I shrug. "Of course." And even though we've just started dating, it totally is. I'm not weirded out at all. Which is … weird. I decide I better not think about it. I'm too tired to actually have any semi-decent relationship analysis right now. Instead, I look down at the book I'm holding. It looks like a math textbook, which—no lie—scares me. "Am I gonna have to multiply and shizzle? Because I'm the worst at—"

"I think you just need to write this formula." Luke points at a long-ass formula in the book that doesn't only have numbers, it has runes.

My eyes roam over the symbols. It's three lines long before the equals sign. My brain shrieks and curls up in a ball, chanting 'not the math, not the math.' I shake my head. "What *is* this?"

"Alchemical equation. It's the same kind of thing wizards use to change substances. Or conceal them."

"So, what do I do?" I ask.

"Just use the marker and write on my hand. Copy that formula."

Luke and I sit back down at my tiny dining table.

I lean over him and hold the sharpie poised. Then, glancing back and forth between the book and Luke, I carefully try to recreate every stroke on the page on Luke's palm. It's frickin' difficult. There are little sun figures and I have to count out how many rays there are before trying to draw tiny triangles. I nearly botch the clover symbol because I start to draw a four-leaf clover instead of a three-leaf. Finally, after ten painstaking minutes, I'm done.

I toss the pen on table and sit back. "I really hope that worked."

Luke puts his temporarily tattooed hand over mine. "I'm sure it did. I have faith in you, Ly."

"Alright, let's test this. You wanna be the Baby Ghoul this time?"

He laughs. "Let's see if it works first. Then, if you are still up for it, I'll let you upstage me as much as you want."

"Deal!"

Luke leans back in his seat, eyes gleaming. "I really really really wanna—"

I wait.

He tries again. No dice. His zigazig ah is still gone.

"Musky tiger balls!" I curse. "Why didn't that work?"

Luke pulls the book toward himself and starts checking my work against what's on the page. When he gets to the clover, he sighs. There is a tiny, miniscule, nearly microscopic dot where I started to draw a four-leaf clover before I realized I didn't need one. Luke points at the dot. "I'm guessing the spellwork is as specific as a hex. Can't have a single piece out of place."

I sink into my chair and sigh. "Sorry. But … what do you know about hexes?"

He shrugs. "Just that they're math like this—what the fuck?"

Luke holds up his left hand, the hand I just wrote that equation on. As we watch, it turns a deep hunter green.

Fear punches me in the gut. "What's happening?"

Luke swallows as he shoves his shirtsleeve back. The green doesn't seem to extend to his arm. It doesn't seem to be spreading. It's just his hand, from the wrist down. He holds his hand up close to his face, examining every detail.

"Is it ... are you part zombie?" I whisper, terrified that I've somehow ruined him. The best guy I've ever dated and I've turned him from the undead into the brainless undead. FML.

Luke turns his hand back and forth. Flexes it. Slams it on the table. That makes me jump. Then he holds it up again and bends each finger one by one. "I don't think it's zombified," he mutters. "But it is ... an interesting side effect to say the least."

"Side effect? I ruined you."

Luke laughs. "Hardly. It's just a little green. Calm down." He pushes his hand toward me. "Tell me what it smells like to you."

I sniff. I pull his hand closer and sniff again. "Is that ... mint?"

He nods. "Kinda faint, right? But, yeah, I thought so, too."

"So, I turned your hand into a mint?"

He stares at his hand again. "Mint plant? Mint relation?" He licks his hand. "Doesn't taste different. I'm not sure. I can still use it. The muscles don't seem affected ... other than being green and the smell."

I grab the book next to him and slam it shut. "Forget this. Flowers can pay a professional and I'll reimburse him for the next five years. We need to get you to a doctor."

"You could just say, 'Luke's hand has lost it' green color.'"

"With the way my stupid power is going, that could take away your entire hand somehow! No! We need a doctor."

Luke shrugs. "Fine. Let's do it tomorrow."

My eyes nearly bug out of my head. "Excuse me, Mr. Green," I gesture wildly at his green hand.

"Yes, Ms. Peacock?"

"This isn't funny. I screwed you up somehow! We need to get it fixed! Ugh."

"You don't like my new green thumb?" Luke grins and holds it up like he's hitchhiking.

"Stop it."

"It feels fine, Ly. Doesn't hurt. Isn't spreading. Let's go to bed and I'll figure it out tomorrow night."

"How can you be so calm about this?"

"Because I've had many magical incidents over the years. This is nothing. Trust me."

I bite my lip.

Luke brings his hands to my shoulders and starts rubbing them. I eye the green hand. "It really is nothing, Ly."

"Text your friend George at least. Make me feel better. Get an appointment for tomorrow."

Luke rolls his eyes but complies. George doesn't have an appointment until two nights from now.

"We need something sooner."

Luke shakes his head. "I promise you; I feel fine. This will be alright. And I trust George."

"I'm coming with you," I tell Luke in my bossiest, most no-nonsense tone.

"Good. We can check on your blood and magic results at the same time."

Right now, that shit is the least of my worries. My powers suck a big one. I don't even want to know what kind of demon I am because I'm kinda mad at whatever kind it is that gave me my shit powers in the first place. If I hadn't fucked up Flowers, I wouldn't have fucked up Luke. I run a tired, angry hand through my hair.

As we head into my bedroom, Luke says, "If I turn all the way green, will you still date me, Ly?"

I growl as I flop onto the bed, fully clothed. "Nope."

Luke jumps onto the bed and makes me bounce. He nuzzles me. "But you did this to me!"

"I know. We're getting it fixed the night after tomorrow," I grumble, snuggling up to my pillow. I don't want to even think about him turning all the way green. That's not gonna happen. Not gonna happen, I repeat in my head, as if making it a mantra will make it come true.

"I dunno if I want this fixed," Luke murmurs. "How intimidating would it be if I keep it in my pocket, but when I get angry, I whip out my green hand, Hulk-style. That could be cool, right?"

"No."

"What about a Green Lantern vibe?"

"Your human is showing."

"Cool Hand Luke?"

"What?"

"Never mind ... ok, non-human. Ninja Turtle? Ichabod the Uruly Troll? Jolly the Green Giant?"

"Maybe." I mumble, just to shut him up.

The last thing I see before I fall asleep is Luke, holding his green hand up in the air and staring at it like it's fascinating or the beginning of something awesome, instead of what I know it is.

It's another mistake by Lyon the loser.

16

I get to work early, before the sun's even down. I hurry, wearing my sleep shirt and some yoga pants for our evening training and tossing other clothes into a duffel. I have to explain everything to Flowers—how I can't do this reversal—and I don't want a showdown in front of peeps.

But when I get inside the gym, Flowers isn't there yet. Bennett is. And he's crying.

He's hunched down on a bench press bench on the far side of the gym, and I can hear his sobs echoing off the walls. My heart cracks in half, just hearing that. I've never seen Bennett look this broken. Not even when we broke up.

I clear my throat, so he'll know I'm there and I make my way over the mats.

"Bennett, what is it?" I ask softly, reaching out to touch his shoulder.

He starts, as if he didn't even notice my throat-clearing, or my walk across the gym. He's so wrapped up in grief he didn't see me. Bennett latches onto my hand and stares up at me with tear-soaked green eyes. "That dragon they found? William? He was a rogue."

A shard of ice forms in my chest. It rips me up. Fuck. Seeing how much this hurts Bennett is just awful.

"There was no one looking for him, Ly. No one cared. Three fucking days he was dead up there. I tried to give him burial rites. But she stole his fucking flame! Louise stole his flame!"

I feel hollow. Disembodied. Stealing a dragon's flame is akin to stealing his soul. I knew Louise took from shifters. Took and sold. But that? Stealing a dragon's core magic to sell it? That was evil incarnate.

"She took his flame ... and no one—" he breaks off. He can't even finish the sentence. His hand nearly crushes mine.

I drop my bags and hug him with my free hand. Bennett drops my other hand and latches onto my waist. I stand there, patting his back and murmuring useless phrases as he buries his face in my stomach. It's a while before he grows quiet. When I feel like he's calm, I tilt his head until he looks up at me. And I give him the one thing I can. "If you ever go missing, I will search for you. I promise."

"You don't—"

"I promise, Bennett," I fasten my eyes on his and don't let him let me off the hook. "You know what a promise means to a fae."

Bennett pulls away and wipes his eyes with the collar of his t-shirt. Then he shakes his head and says, "Ly, I don't think that's a good idea."

"Bennett French!" I scoop up my bag and whack him with it. Because, heartbroken or not, he needs to hear me and get this through his thick dragon skull. "You are clan to me. We were friends first. Things might be weird now. But we'll be friends again. And if you need me, I expect a darn phone call. No more avoiding my texts either, young man."

Bennett gives me a weak grin. "Are you channeling Sarah Snow right now?"

"Maybe?" I shrug and give a snorty little laugh. "They're clan, too."

Bennett sniffs. "What you're doing is nice. But it's not the same."

"I know it's not. I'm not a dragon. I'm apparently, probably, maybe, part demon. So, it's the best I've got. You. Me. Tabby. Sarah. Jacob. JR. Got it?"

Bennett nods. "Are you sure they're gonna want—"

"Shut your flaming trap," I tell him. "Tabby's loved you since the moment she saw you half shift on my balcony. I wouldn't be surprised if she doesn't spy on you regularly with her crystal—"

"WHAT?"

Ah crap. I almost outed Tabby's illegal crystal ball spying practice. Crud. "I mean … I'm pretty sure she's got some pictures of you taped to her crystal mirror."

Bennett narrows his eyes.

"Think of her as the dirty old step-aunt you never wanted."

Bennett puts a hand over his face and groans. "Ly, why?"

"See? That face! That right there! That's true family annoyance going on already! Admit it. We're clan to you, too. You can even vent about me to JR. She's always wanted someone to vent to. I mean, when you're best friends with this," I gesture up and down at myself as cockily as I can, "it can get a little rough."

Bennett gives me the grin I was looking for. He swipes at his face one last time. "I'll think about it."

"Too late. Done is done. If you reject us, I'll tell Blue Snow Matchmaking to make you their next victim."

"That's blackmail!"

I shrug. "Not when it's between family."

Bennett shakes his head and stands. "I'm leaving, before you start spouting off some other craziness."

"It's called wisdom, Bennett French."

"That's wisdom?" he scoffs.

"Yup. You probably have forgotten what it looks like since you've been spending so much time with Flowers—"

"What was that?" a voice behind me asks.

I half turn and cringe. There, in all his muscled, perfectly combed and groomed early evening glory, is Flowers. And he's glaring down at me like I'm the nose hair that didn't get trimmed but was discovered in the office bathroom mirror— right before the big presentation. Snarling tiger cubs! Why'd he have to walk up right then? Huh? Why?

But then—the world flips on its end. Day becomes night. Night becomes day.

Flowers. Goes. Nuts.

He leans into me and suddenly rubs his nose along my spine. He takes a big inhale. And then he scoops me up and drops me face first on the practice mat, pouncing on me and rubbing his cheek into my back.

I screech, "Ahh! What the—"

Thank goodness Bennett's there to witness the madness and save me. He yanks Flowers off me. "What the hell, man?"

But Flowers is jumpy, hyper. He wiggles in Bennett's grasp as I sit up, batting at the dragon-shifter's hands. "Lemme go. Lemme go. Just another smell."

I stand and exchange a concerned look with Bennett. "What's his problem?"

Bennett struggles with Flowers, who's kicking like a crazy man. I jump forward to try to help Bennett pin him down and Flowers just starts grinning. And purring. Right at me. Whiskers sprout from his cheeks. His ears start to turn orange and furry.

"Crud! He's shifting, Bennett!" I yell. This isn't Flowers. Whatever's going on, this is not the shifter I've come to know and hate. This is weird ass, what-the-hell kinda shit going down. I think Flowers might be ... high.

Flowers eyes flicker back and forth between human and cat.

"If he fully shifts, get out—" Bennett doesn't get to finish the sentence before Flowers wriggles out of his grasp and grabs me again.

Flowers pulls me to the floor mats and climbs on top of me. Then he flips me over and starts deliberately rubbing his forehead into my shirt. "Smells soo good." I'm being assaulted by an oversized cat shifter who's high.

That thought triggers something. Darrell was assaulted by cats, too. Cat shifters get high … on catnip.

WTF? Why do I smell like catnip? I don't have cats. Can't keep a plant alive … but then my mind goes to Luke's green hand. The minty one. We slept snuggled up together. Fuck!

I suck in a breath and yank off my shirt. (Good thing I wore my good sports bra today and not the one with the hole in it.) I toss the shirt across the room. "Let him go!"

Bennett looks at me like I'm crazy. But Flowers immediately redirects his flailing from me to the shirt. Bennett lets him go. Flowers bounds after the shirt and wraps it around his face. He nuzzles the shirt, chews on it. He bounces around the room on his hands and feet with my shirt between his teeth.

I chuckle and reach into my bag. I pull out my phone instead of the replacement shirt I was initially gonna grab because … well, isn't it obvious? Some things take priority. Recording this event is one of them.

I've hardly hit record before Bennett's hand stops me. "Don't. Get dressed."

"But—"

Bennett shakes his head. He doesn't look amused. He looks sad. "Flowers' mom was addicted to nip. It's why he's so …"

My stomach sinks as every uptight piece of Flowers' personality gets put into perspective. And now I feel like a jerk. I grab my other shirt out of the duffel and toss it on. "Oh."

"Why does your shirt smell like catnip?"

Crap! That makes me do a double take. Luke! He's at my place. And Tabby had invited a bunch of her cat shifter friends … I grab my phone and run outside without answering Bennett. I Faceshrine Luke.

"Hey, I think your hand isn't mint. It's catnip!" I tell him as soon as he answers.

Luke raises an eyebrow. "Yeah, kinda already figured it out." He pulls the phone away from himself and I see four cats crawling all over his lap as he sits on the exterior steps of my apartment building. The light from my porch outlines him and the cats in the darkness. Tabby's notched ear and orange fur stand out from the crowd. She nuzzles his armpit.

"That's a whole lotta ancient puss—" I can't say it.

"Ha ha," Luke responds. He sneezes. "Of course, it had to be catnip. Did you know, I'm allergic to cats?"

"Bad allergic?"

"Nah. Just sneezy. Watery eyes."

I give him a tight grin. "Well then, I'll leave you to your clowder of cats."

I move my hand to the red button just as Luke says, "Wait—how did you figure out that my hand smells like catnip?"

I chicken out and press the red button instead of answering. I do not feel like telling my new boyfriend I found out about catnip because I was tackled by a tiger-shifter.

17

Flowers shakes off his high after about ten minutes. My shirt is completely shredded before then. Of course, he comes barreling at me as soon as he's in his right mind.

"What the -uck? What the hell was that?"

I sigh. Of course, he thinks I did this on purpose.

Bennett intervenes. I explained everything to him while we waited for Flowers' tail to recede. (BTW, watching a guy partially shift and a tiger tail shoot down out of the bottom of his shorts is both shocking and oddly satisfying.)

Once Bennett gets Flowers' immediate urge to blame and rage at me under control, talk turns back to the case at hand.

Seena comes in early and we all end up discussing Louise Grant. Even though Bennett's technically not overseeing the case, he says, "Well, have you guys talked to that Francis Dogle—Hopper—whatever his name is?"

"On tonight's list," Flowers glowers. I can't tell if he's back to his regular grumpy self or annoyed that Bennett is trying to nudge him about the case.

Bennett nods. "Well, if you want me to take over the training, you could take these two with you …"

Flowers sighs but nods. I'm sure he'd rather poke a stick in his eye than take me, but you don't argue with the boss. We all trudge out of the gym as the other Academy recruits come piling in.

Seena whispers to me, "Why's he so grumpy?"

I just shrug. No way I'm letting rumors get around about the catnip thing.

We get to the address we got from Frank the hippo. It's a decent townhouse with a lot of tall trees and a savannah style park with a zebra mom and her kid wandering through it.

The townhouse we park in front of is a bit dingier than the rest. It has several trees stripped of leaves and the windows are streaky with dirt or something. We go up to the front door and knock. Then we ring the bell. There's no answer, though we can hear the TV on inside. Flowers sighs and grabs his cell. He walks down the steps to call a judge so we can try to get a warrant. But then Seena tries the doorknob. It's unlocked. He pushes open the door and calls into the front hall, "Hello?"

The inside of the townhouse is nicer than I expect. It has super tall ceilings and plush carpet. A giraffe head pops around the corner. Its eyes widen and the long purple tongue snakes out of its mouth when it spots us.

"Can we come in?" I ask the giraffe. "Just looking for Hopper." Then I second guess myself. I assumed this was a shifter. But what if it's not? What if it's just a giraffe.

I'm about to face palm when the giraffe's mouth opens. It looks like the giraffe is trying to speak, but I can't hear anything. I turn to Seena. "Does the handbook say we need verbal confirmation in order to enter?"

He nods. "Verbal or visual." He lets his ears shift to horse ears and he flicks them back and forth on the side of his head.

"Is, is the giraffe talking?" I ask.

Seena holds up a hand to tell me to shut it. I do. He asks again if we can come in and says, "I need a head nod."

The giraffe gives a slow nod.

Seena grins and then lets his ears shift to human again before he calls out to Flowers, "Permission to enter granted, sir!"

Flowers comes up the stairs muttering about judges and incompetence and stomps right past us toward the giraffe in the living room. He doesn't offer so much as a 'hello.'

But he stops short when we turn the corner and see the giraffe isn't just a giraffe. She's got giant, electric blue butterfly wings. The pattern from her wings extends onto the spots on her torso, which are also dazzling blue. Her legs wobble and draw my eye downward. That's when I realize ... she's chained to the wall at the ankle.

"Cat whiskers!" I whisper.

Flowers immediately gets to work freeing her. He's got a handy little metal-eating potion in a vial on his tactical belt that he rubs onto the chain. A couple seconds later, the butterfly giraffe walks free as Seena and I take video and photos with our phone—the one downside of the potion is that it will eat the chains until there's nothing left.

The butterfly giraffe stumbles into a nearby bedroom. A few seconds later, a woman in her early twenties, with bright red hair and a neck full of tattoos emerges, cinching a short silk robe with short sleeves around her waist.

My jaw drops. I fumble for my purse. I pull out those missing person fliers I picked up. I hold up the black and white photocopy and stare. "Are you ... Rachel?"

The woman blinks at me. "Yeah. Do I know you?"

I shake my head. "People are looking for you." I show her the flier.

Flowers grabs it out of my hand and scans it. Then he looks up at Rachel. "Why were you chained up?"

"Hopper's an asshole," she shrugs, as if getting chained up is no big deal.

"I'm sorry, what?" Seena says.

Rachel just grins and uses a hair tie on her arm to toss her hair into a messy bun. "He's an asshole and an idiot. I dunno what you're after him for, but if you catch that dimwit trying to sell shifter pee … just know it wasn't given willingly and mine's not gonna do jack shit."

Everything this woman just said is confusing me. There's only one thing in the world that makes sense right now. She's a redhead. And she has the initials EWNM tattooed on her neck.

AFTER I POINT OUT THE TATTOO, FLOWERS ESCORTS RACHEL downtown for questioning. We learn the following:

1. She's been dating Hopper aka Francis Dogle aka Grasshorse for a couple months.

2. He's killer in the sack but sucks at life in general.

3. She has an amazing tattoo artist named Grendel, who she swears can make birds fly up and down your skin. (I write his name down.)

3. Hopper overheard her talking to some friends she refuses to name, about the chemical properties of mixed shifter urine.

Apparently, it was this last item that prompted Hopper to chain her up and make her pee in a jar. Then he left the house a few nights ago, no explanation.

"Next time I see that bastard, I'm gonna snap his—"

"Might not want to finish that sentence in here," Seena warns her, gesturing to the cops outside the meeting room. Flowers decided to give Rachel the kid glove treatment, since he thinks she's more of a witness than a suspect, even though she was seen arguing with Louise the night of her death.

I've been sitting in the corner, drinking coffee and letting Seena and Flowers play good cop/bad cop and just trying to put the pieces together.

Seena finally builds up to asking, "How did you know Louise Grant?"

"Bitch used to be our supplier."

I do a double take. Is Rachel dumb enough to admit to selling Nappies? She doesn't seem like it but… "Your dealer?" I ask.

"No! Supplier for work. Until someone let it slip that mixed shifter urine is like one of the best erasers on the planet."

"Wait, what?" Seena holds up a hand. "Can you explain that?"

"I don't get all the alchemical math—that's Mar—" she cuts herself off and redirects the conversation. "Look, the point is, if you have two completely opposite shifters, a pred and a prey mixed, like a zebra lion or something—they cancel each other out. Erase one another's power. Somehow that gets into their pee."

Flowers sits back in his seat. For some reason, he looks over at me. I'm not a frickin' mixed shifter. I'm definitely not an expert on power, or alchemical equations. Luke's green catnip hand can testify to that. All I know is that mixed magic kinda sucks.

I kinda feel like Flowers is waiting for me to talk, because he doesn't stop looking. The pressure builds the longer he stares. I clear my throat and ask, "Just out of curiosity, what's the tattoo on your neck stand for?"

Rachel touches the letters on her neck. "Oh, there's a group of us that got them when we turned eighteen. Evil, Wicked, Nasty, Mean." She touches the tattoo on her neck nostalgically.

"Any reason for it?"

She shrugs, "That's the real world isn't it? The second you forget that, it gut punches you."

I nod and decide she's warmed up enough that I can switch topics. (See … that Academy training is learning me good.) "Why pee? Why not blood or hair or something else?"

"Didn't I just say I'm not a, like, alchemical equation guru? I don't know!" Rachel sits back, crossing her arms and glaring at me.

"Why were you arguing with Louise Grant the other night?" I already know they were arguing about money. But I want to see what Rachel says.

"Because I know that bitch knows where Bill is," Rachel bursts out before snapping her lips together and glaring hard at me.

Interesting. She didn't mean to say that. She didn't want to say that. Why? Who's Bill?

"Bill? I thought you were arguing about unpaid bills. You said she was your supplier, right?" I go for stupid and casual. Obviously, Lilypunt, who overheard the fight, thought that.

"Bill was our delivery guy. Ran urine from Louise's to our building. And he never came back." My gut starts to tingle.

"When was the last time you saw him?" Seena asks.

But I'm zoned out of the conversation. I'm scooping up my purse from the floor, burrowing into it, and pulling out that second flier. The boy-next-door who was missing. Bill. I hold up the flier. "Is this your Bill?" I ask, handing the flier over so Rachel can see it.

"Yeah." Rachel says, staring down at the flier. "So, nobody's found him? Even while I was chained up?"

Flowers takes the flier casually from her and glances at it. Then he clears his throat and says, "Lyon, can we step into the hall -or a minute?"

I nod and follow him out as Seena asks for timeline details from Rachel for the day of Louise Grant's murder.

Once the door is shut, I lean against it. "Yes?"

Flowers holds up the flier. "Where'd you get this?"

I shrug. "Local cleaner near my house. I guess one of their friends must have put them up at shops, looking for Rachel and Bill. Why?"

Flowers holds up the flier. "Because this is William Henson. The dragon who was dead at Louise's place."

I swallow hard and my stomach drops. Rachel the redhead was friends with Bill. Bill was the delivery boy for Louise's. Bill is dead. Rachel was arguing with Louise about Bill the night Louise died. Crap. I glance inside the meeting room. I stare hard at Rachel. Could she be the killer?

Next to me, Flowers sighs. "Looks like we just discovered the best motive -or murder." He doesn't sound triumphant about it. I mean, if Rachel is the murderer, and she killed Louise

Grant, the pee and blood sweat and dragon-fire stealing, body-hiding dealer ... I guess there's not much to be triumphant about. But, something about Rachel doesn't scream murderer to me.

"She says she doesn't understand alchemical equations, though," I point out.

"Says doesn't mean a whole lot. We can place her at the scene just be-ore ... beshore the crime. She's got a shit ton o-motive, considering Louise killed her thriend.'" Flowers stumbles through those sentences with only a mild glare. Guess he's adjusting to his lisp. Or maybe he's just confident that some doc at the hospital will be able to reverse my idiocy.

I smack my wayward thoughts and turn them back to Rachel. I make them think through more reasons she might not have been able to commit the crime. "She's been chained up for two nights!"

Flowers purses his lips. "Again, so she says. We need to get her boy toy, and question him, too. He was there that night."

"He was in a cage when we found him."

Flowers shrugs. "Hopper's shithter animal is small. He could have slipped in and out."

"Why stay? The doors and windows in that place were all open. If they killed Louise, running is the cleanest option, isn't it? And, wasn't Hopper still high when we got there?"

"Could have taken the Nappies athter … once it was done."

"But that hex was fresh. The milk in the carton was still cold," I point out. "Louise just poured it, cut herself with the knife while she was chopping those veggies, and was walking to the door—probably because she heard you—when she tunked over dead."

Flowers fingers come up and flex. Like he wants to choke me out. "Sometimes, I think you just want to argue just to argue."

"Maybe. But not this time. I think you're wrong."

Flowers shakes his head. "Prove it."

He shoves open the door and tells Seena to read Rachel her rights.

I stand outside in the hall. The gauntlet has been thrown. The need to prove Flowers wrong is visceral. It's like a writhing snake in my stomach. But, is he wrong? What do I have to go on?

How the claw paw am I gonna prove it?

18

Rachel gets dragged off to booking kicking and screaming, her red hair flying everywhere. She's so pissed her neck starts to elongate even though she doesn't fully shift. "If you want a damned criminal, look at Hopper! I bet that ass is trying to sell my urine right now!" She stretches her neck around the corner so she can glare at us a second longer before she's dragged off to booking.

Seena just rolls his eyes.

But her outburst makes me sit down in one of the million chairs set around the open layout of the station. The senior officer working at the desk in front of me looks up, but I ignore him. My thoughts are too busy swarming. I feel like answers are just out of reach, and they're bugging me, like bees buzzing around my head.

I wonder where the hell you go to sell urine. I have no clue, having never known that's a disgusting-ass, real-world thing. There are black markets. But our officers regularly patrol the known ones. I'd think the urine thing would come up in training if the urine thing was widespread.

So, I wander around, go upstairs and head back to our main offices, and somehow, I end up perched on JR's desk. Arnold's out today, thank goodness, so I don't have to stare at his hairy werewolf tail while I ask JR who might possibly purchase shifter pee.

The face I get when I ask her that is the perfect comical, nose-scrunching, stuck-out-tongue disgusted face. "Oh my stars, why would I know that? That's just plain horrific."

"Apparently, when pee comes from a mixed shifter then it's got a magical nullifying effect—"

"I just heard blah-blah-blah gross."

I sigh and put my head in my hands. "I know. Me too. I really don't get this stuff. I mean, I'd be a terrible witch. Don't they have to learn all this stuff?"

JR shrugs. "Yeah. I think Alchemy is part of the curriculum at the high school. Why don't you ask Luke? Isn't he king of the nerdy sciencey shit?"

I kiss her on top of her head and muss her librarian-style bun. "You're a genius."

"Obviously not, otherwise I'd know all about shifter urine."

"What's that?" Liza, one of the older female werewolf paralegals, stops and asks.

"Do you sell your urine?" I question. "Or know anyone who would buy or sell it?"

Liza's face mimic's JR's. "Um, no. That's weird. Only thing I can think people would buy urine for is to mark their boundaries. Like … if they wanted a stronger alpha scent to keep people out. Like, ranchers trying to keep us away from their sheep on the full moon. That kinda thing."

I chew my lip. Hmmm… definitely not what I think mixed shifter urine does. I brainstorm as I walk down the stairs and outside. I decide I need a little churro at the snack cart in order to bolster myself.

The little furry green gremlin working the cart winks and gives me an extra churro, which cheers me up considerably.

I call Luke, who's on his lunch break. "What's up, beautiful?"

"I have very strange questions for you. If you're drinking, you might want to pause," I tell him as I crunch down on my churro.

"You're eating through this conversation," he points out. "But I can't drink?"

"I'm being considerate. I've been thinking about pee for the last three hours and so now I'm kinda immune to the gross factor."

I hear Luke sigh, and then a small noise like he might be sliding a cup away from him. "You know, this is not the kind of dirty conversation I'd hoped you were calling me to have."

"Trust me, it's not the kind of conversation I want to have either. I can't give you details, but, like, I'm wondering about pee."

"Okay?" I hear the smile in Luke's voice. "It's a natural bodily function—"

"Wait. Wait. I mean mixed shifter pee."

"Ahhh," Luke's tone tells me that there is something going on with shifter urine. "Is there somewhere I can meet you in person?"

Confusion fills my head like cream injected into a donut. Why would he want to meet me to talk about pee? "I'm outside in front of the courthouse. You don't have to—"

"Be right there."

There's a *whoosh* and then a dial tone.

I sit back with my churro. Five bites later, Luke's standing in front of me, hair windblown but he's not even winded. Damn vampire. I got out of workouts this evening, but I do not look all glamorous and shit when I'm done with them.

Generally, I look like a slippery, sweaty red tomato. How dare he look hot!

Luke leans forward and sniffs my churro. "Mmmm."

I grin up at him and take a bite. "You know what I just realized? You might be the perfect guy. You approve of all my junk food, but don't steal it."

Luke laughs. "You're just realizing this?"

I shrug. "I'm slow. This is why I'm so confused by this pee thing. I didn't know mixed shifter pee was a thing. I mean … gross."

"Didn't we talk about it the other day when you went to pick up your uniform?" Luke sits down next to me on one of the crappy concrete benches set outside the courthouse. He eyes a tentacled attorney who's arguing with a client across the way.

"What? No."

"Oh, I thought I told you that's why I didn't like the idea of you going to the dry cleaners. They use mixed shifter urine."

"WHAT?" That comes out really loud. I mean, like echo-across-the-courtyard loud. I cringe as strangers stop to stare. I give one of those pathetic apology waves, hide my face behind a curtain of hair and turn into Luke. "What do you mean the dry cleaners use urine?"

237

"Urine's been a cleaner for centuries. The ammonia in it. Humans used it for years. They have transitioned over to chemicals over the past fifty years, horrid chemicals by the way—so don't go taking your clothes there either—but shifter urine's … stronger." Luke shrugs.

"You're saying that when I take my clothes to get dry cleaned, I'm actually getting them sprayed with shifter pee?"

"Um … yeah?"

I shudder. "That is so disgusting!" My stomach twists and I have to hand the churro to Luke. I thought I had a handle on this pee topic. Apparently not. I have to shake my hands out just thinking about it. I thought dry cleaning was some magical spell kinda thing-a-ma-jig. Wave of the wand and bam! Nope. Crapola. Now I'm gonna burn all of my nice clothes. A thought occurs to me though. I used to wear suits more when I worked as a paralegal. And I was in an office full of shifters because Arnold is a favoritism-type of furry butt. "Wait … why didn't anyone at my old office smell it on me?"

Luke raises an eyebrow. "This is where your question about mixed shifter pee becomes relevant. The right mixes cancel out any scent and any magic. They effectively erase each other."

"Like a magic eraser?"

"Yup."

I sit there and mull that over. "Why did you want to come talk to me about this in person?"

Luke glances around and then looks at me. "Who do you think uses magic erasers?"

"Dry cleaners, obviously."

"Some house cleaners, too," he adds, ignoring my look of disgust. "And …" Luke just stares steadily at me.

I can't believe it takes a minute. But it slams into like a freight train. Who would want a magic eraser? Who would want to get rid of magic? People who did it illegally. "Criminals. But we haven't studied this! I mean … if this is a thing, wouldn't the cops know?"

"What if it's a relatively new thing? At least as far as I know."

"What do you mean?"

"I mean, sometimes when one goes to dinner at one's mother's house … one overhears things. Nothing incriminating," he's quick to add, "I might have interrupted what could have been a very innocent discussion of proper cleaning techniques and how expensive cleaning products have gotten." The sarcasm in Luke's tone tells me all I need to know. The convo might have been innocent on the surface, but he knows what it implied. At the same time, he doesn't want to get pulled in for questioning about his mom.

I don't blame him. His mom is one scary lady. I press my lips together. I don't want to have to go shake down Cookie Gonzalez and the Crypts. Just because things ended well once does not mean she'd be lenient again.

"So, the Crypts are using magic erasers …" I mutter, half to myself.

But Luke and his damn vamp hearing overhear. "They aren't the only ones. The Bloods might be slower … but they always get there." His kiss on my cheek is swift. "I gotta get back to work."

He's gone before I can blink. And he took my churro!

I can't even curse him in my head though. My mind is too full. Too blown.

My thoughts bounce around. No wonder Louise had jars of piss at her house. I wonder how much mixed shifter pee goes for. Did her boss know? Who bought Louise's jars of pee? Cleaners seem unlikely. She supposedly worked for the Bloods, the local troll gang. Not the brightest. But hella violent. If Luke's saying the Bloods use magic eraser pee too, then maybe Louise was hoarding it for them. Or selling it to them. But what kind of magic would the Bloods want to hide? And would Louise know what it was? Would they have killed her to try and get those jars? Or so they didn't have to pay her for them? Or was she selling them to the Crypts and the Bloods found out and whacked her for it?

If the Bloods whacked her, why didn't they erase the hex if they knew about Magic Erasers? (I've decided that's my new euphemism. I'm just gonna forget that this is about urine.) My gut says it's because we interrupted the murderer. That the killer was someone who was there that night. Because they didn't take the Magic Erasers with them. Could it be Rachel then? Is Flowers right?

I can't pinpoint why, but my gut says no. Somehow, I don't see her giraffe butterfly shifter form making a quick getaway. Plus, she just doesn't seem that quick-thinking. She let herself get chained up. And though I can see how she could get talked into that one by her boy toy... I still don't think she did this. My gut says that there's some missing piece to this puzzle.

If it wasn't Rachel, who offed Louise?

No matter how I slice it, it seems like all my questions point to the Bloods for more answers.

I think it might be time to visit Louise's boss: Tar.

But you don't take pixie dust to a wand fight. And you don't walk into Troll territory alone.

I'm gonna need backup.

19

lowers rolls his eyes when I say I want to go to the
Blood's main nightclub, the Tar Pit, but he agrees
to go with me when I say it's the most likely place
Hopper will be selling that urine.

He rounds up Petey, for the vamp's compulsion abilities. To
my shock, little tiny Becca wants to go, too.

"I've never seen the Tar Pit," she says as she grabs her jacket.
"It's supposed to be super exclusive. And the owner is like a
recluse. No one ever sees him. Total intrigue. On that case
Petey and I were assigned, that troll supposedly smashed up
an underground fight scene that went down there. But we
got reassigned to your case before we ever got to go to the
Tar Pit. They just rebuilt it. It's supposed to be epic. Plus …
there's supposed to be an FFA fight this weekend. I bet that

place is gonna be full of ripped, shirtless FFA-style supernaturals. I mean, droolfest."

Seena glares at her from his desk, his glasses sliding down his nose. "Excuse me, the droolfest is right here, thank you very much." He gestures at himself in his pressed pink checkered shirt, and slightly cowlicky black hair.

Becca leans down and ruffles his hair. "Oh, trust me, I know." She winks at him.

Seena mutters, "Ungrateful sprite," as we walk toward the stairwell. He rolls his eyes and grins as Becca blows him a kiss.

Flowers pushes open the door only to run into Bennett, nearly knocking the dragon shifter down the stairs.

"Whoa! Sorry, Boss," Flowers reaches out and pulls Bennett up by the shoulder.

Bennett eyes our group. "What's going on?"

"We're going to the Tar Pit!" Becca's giddy. I mean, she's always bubbly, but she must really have a thing for trolls because this is just odd.

Bennett's eyes narrow and land on me. "I'm coming with you."

Awkward. "We'll be fine—"

But he doesn't even acknowledge me. He just backs up and holds open the door to the stairs so that we all have to squeeze past him. Unfortunately, I'm last in line.

"This dumb idea was yours, wasn't it?" Bennett whispers as we traipse down the stairs.

"It isn't dumb. We know Louise was selling urine to erase magic. The Bloods make the most sense as buyers."

"Figuring that out isn't the dumb part. The idea that you're gonna confront them about it is the dumb part."

I stop walking and glare back at him. "I'm not gonna confront them! I'm just gonna try and catch them in the act!"

"Nights after the crime?"

"Hopper's got that can of pee. And we can see if someone's heard about the dragon fire."

"Sometimes I think you have a death wish."

"Solving a crime is a death wish?"

"You have been known to run off after murderers by yourself."

I grit my teeth. "I was rescuing my mother."

"And the concert? Where you chased what's-her-name?"

What the hell? Why is he picking on me? "We were *all* chasing her!"

"And what about dating the son of a gang leader?"

I whirl on Bennett. "You are about this close to losing your invite to Thanksgiving dinner this year!"

"Are you cooking?"

"Hell no. I plan to force Jacob to come back for a visit so he can cook."

Bennett rolls his eyes and just stomps past me.

I stare at his back and shake my head. That was aggressive. Bennett doesn't do aggressive. Not in the asshole way Flowers does. I think he's still upset about that dragon. William ... I mean Bill.

But I don't really know what to do about that. Best I can do is try to help him find that dragon fire so we can put the poor guy to rest.

One uncomfortable car ride later, we pull up into a parking lot full of open-air jeeps, the only vehicles full trolls can fit in since they are seven to nine feet tall. The Tar Pit is a giant warehouse. The roll up garage doors are a better size for customers, I think as I eye the black metal exterior. Not to mention how violent trolls are. It wouldn't be worth it to buy real building for trolls to dance in. I can see a few new panels on one wall. I guess that's what Becca was talking about when she said they had to fix this place up.

I shake my head and remind myself not to do anything offensive. Even as we walk up, I hear body clanging against the metal siding of the warehouse. Maybe someone's drink was mixed wrong. Doesn't take much to set a troll off.

"Okay, everyone, we're gonna look for Hopper or Tar or anyone with a jar of urine or dragon fire," I say as we get close.

Flowers rolls his eyes at me trying to take charge; Bennett's face is dark; Petey bites his lip; Becca presses her hands together like she's so excited she can hardly contain herself. (I swear that sprite is happy about everything.)

We get past the bouncer no problem until it comes to Becca. The bouncer looks part troll himself at 6'5", but he has enough good sense to say, in a deep silky voice, "You gonna get squished in there, little lady."

Becca shoots back, "I will not!"

He shakes his head, his five nose rings jingling as he smiles and says, "Sorry. But the boss won't let me let in dwarves."

So … um … fact: dwarves are not attractive. They are a race with squat figures and a lot of facial hair. Becca is a stick thin water sprite. She starts to steam as she stares this bouncer down.

Suddenly, the bouncer turns red as a watermelon. The guy starts choking. He starts spitting up the massive amounts of water.

Bennett grabs Becca by the shoulder. "Stop!"

She shrugs and grudgingly makes the bouncer stop choking. The guy takes a swipe at her. My eyes widen in horror. I'm about to see little Becca get crushed by a part-troll. WTF? How am I gonna tell Seena?

But, as the guy's hand reaches her head, Becca turns into water. Her body suddenly liquefies. She morphs into a swirling mass of water shaped like a person. Her clothes spin around like they're in an upright washing machine. Her skirt spirals up through her stomach and behind her blinking eyes, that somehow, are still eyes. (Magic is weird.) I try to ignore the fact that her whirling thong gets caught along her shoulder. The point is —the bouncer's hand passes right through her.

Instead of screaming and stomping like I expect him to, the troll just laughs. "Okay, fine, little lady, you proved your point. Go on in with your friends."

Becca slowly solidifies her arms first, yanking her clothes back into place so she's covered as the rest of her body goes back to normal.

Bennett and Flowers both eye her with envy.

"Wish I could do that," Bennett grumbles, no doubt thinking of all the clothes he's shredded when shifting.

Becca shakes a head as her teeth start chattering. Her clothes are still soaked. "It's awesome during summer. Now? Not so much."

Bennett lets out a smoke ring or two and Becca steps into the heat to dry off. "Thanks, Commander."

We head through the door and I can't help but give Becca a pat on the back. "I had no idea you were such a reaper. Life-endingly cool, lady."

She grins over at me. "I might have dated a troll or two in my day. You have to line those suckers out. Don't tell Seena."

We get inside and instead of fog and strobe lights, there's sulfur and black lights that highlight the trolls' teeth, making everything stuck between said teeth that much more visible. Of course, trolls grow fungus on their teeth on purpose, kinda like some humans put gold in their teeth on purpose. They think it's hot. Part of me wonders if the sulfuric smell in here is caused by their bad breath.

"Let's break into two groups. Flowers, you take point on the left side I'll take point on the right side," Bennett orders, immediately going into commander mode.

Flowers and Petey head off in one direction. I follow behind Bennett with Becca. It's hard to see through the crowds since they are so tall, but I keep my eyes peeled because my intuition is pinging.

Something's about to happen here, I can feel it.

We make our way toward the trolls' dance floor. Only they don't dance on a wooden floor. The name of this place is not creative—it's literal.

Trolls bump and grind while their feet are stuck in three inches of black sludgy tar. The theory is that the tar is supposed to slow them down in case of a fight. Plus, they supposedly love the feel of the thick sticky goo. (They have notoriously dry cracked skin. Like Grand Canyon style crevices when they don't exfoliate.)

Two blue trolls are out-dancing everyone around them. Their hands whip up and down like jumping jacks and they bob their heads.

"Ooh, they're doing the flap!" Becca says as she starts to do it too, smacking me in the waist as she tries to imitate a bird, her neck jutting forward with each flap of her arms.

"Do I want to know how you know this dance?" I asked.

"Nope. Ooh! Look at those hotties!" Becca points to a group of guys standing outside the nasty black tar goo. Each one of them is sporting arms as big as fifty-year old tree trunks. They are ripped, in a way that moves past hot into scary. Or maybe it's the fact that they all have shaved heads and have metal spikes implanted on different parts of their skulls that makes them scary.

The nightmarish group is all huddled together and talking quietly.

Becca walks straight toward them, flipping her hair behind her back. "Hey guys," she grins.

I hang back, letting a couple people get between me and her. I'm not sure what her plan is, but even I wouldn't just walk up to these iron-heads. I peer through the crowd, hoping Bennett's noticed we aren't behind him.

Nope. No luck. But then I see Flowers heading our way. So, I feel a little less likely to die in the next two seconds.

Until Becca says, "So, who's been trying to sell you guys urine tonight?" She says it casually, as if she's asking about the score of a game.

The guys stiffen. One of them, with a spike coming out the bottom of his nose, growls, "What?"

Becca gives a wry grin, completely unintimidated. "Please. You don't expect me to believe you aren't juicing. Come on. We all know Ironmen causes hair loss."

"We shave our heads!" a yellow dude with a head full of horned spikes says. "So no one can pull our hair."

"Sure, you do," Becca grins. "Because so many of your opponents are eight feet tall and can reach that head of yours."

(Side note: I'm kind of in awe of her fearlessness.)

"Look guys, I can take you all downtown and you can take turns peeing in cups with a little friend of mine watching to

251

ensure you don't mix in any shifter pee … or you can point me in the direction of the person who 'attempted'"—her air quotes reek of sarcasm—"to sell you urine so you'd pass your tests tomorrow."

The trolls exchange a glance. Then they step apart to reveal Hopper. I'd thought that dude had been huge the night we found him at the nap shack. But, next to these guys, he looks tiny. His legs aren't as thick as their arms. His green mohawk doesn't even reach their shoulders.

Becca steps up to Hopper without an ounce of hesitation. She pulls out her cuffs just as Bennett joins us.

One of the other trolls growls and reaches toward Becca, but a huge shadow falls across our group. Gasps go up around us.

I look up to see a troll who's so tall he has to duck his head to speak to us. His voice grumbles like rocks tumbling through a polisher.

"What seems to be the trouble here?" he asks.

"Tar," one of the trolls gives a respectful snarl to the side, eyes downcast to show his subservience.

So, this is Tar. Louise's boss. One of the Bloods. Tar Pit. I thought this was just named for the dance floor. But is this his place?

Camera phones are coming out. Like seeing him is a big deal or something. Didn't Becca say the owner was a recluse?

I eye the troll that's so large he's clothed in cloth tarps. He's got to be at least ten feet tall. He could crack my skull in one hand. Possibly Becca's too, at the same time. This does not make me feel good.

His skin is baby-smooth and a pale yellow that glows nicely under the black lights. He has only minimal dandruff, which is saying something, for a troll.

Becca eyes Tar with disdain. "Look what the giant dragged in."

Tar laughs. "Still bitter about the breakup, princess?"

I cannot control my jaw. It flips down and refuses to shut as I gape at the two of them. They dated? Becca dated *him*?

"It's not called bitterness. It's more 'I'm damn glad you hired a half-wit witch doctor and the love spell wore off.' So … you're heading up Nappie dealers now that you made it big-time huh? Now that the Bloods let you in so you could be their little bitch?"

I catch Bennett's eye—he's finally freaking noticed we're gone and is heading back—and I give him a little 'what the hell do we do' look. I know I'm not supposed to back away from Becca. We're on assignment. That would show weakness. We have to put on a united front as cops. But what the mother-loving heck? She's gonna get us obliterated.

Becca's on a roll. She just keeps going, laying into Tar. "Bet momma's proud of you. Following her footsteps. Turning into a criminal who steals from people who're helpless babies."

Tar shoves his face down at Becca. His fists curl and his nostrils flare. His eyebrows crunch together to form one solid line. Those—according to a very detailed illustration on page 527 of our training manual—are clear signs he's about to fight.

Screw protocol. I'm not quite ready to die. I shuffle back a couple steps and bump into someone in a cloak. Someone short enough to be human.

"Sorry," I start—

But then the world is engulfed in white heat. And all I have time to register is Becca dropping to the floor in a steaming puddle and Bennett, suddenly next to me and going dragon, wings lifting up to shield me from the massive wall of white heat.

"What the hopping mad cats was that?" I ask, when Bennett finally releases me from the shelter of his black wingspan.

Bennett doesn't answer as he struggles to shove a flame into a spelled bottle with his claws. His black dragon nostrils snort smoke.

Around me, everyone looks dazed as the smoke clears. The trolls Becca was harassing are black, their skin cracked like burnt wood.

"Ugh," one groans. "Look at me!" He eyes a huge crevice in the skin of his arm. "That's basically a handhold for a fae now." Luckily, troll skin is crazy thick, it only looks like these guys got surface burns. Hopper is … nowhere to be found.

That little green dick! Did he throw fire at us to try to escape?

I whirl around, looking for him, only to run into Becca's waves as she stands up, still liquid. She blinks at me and speaks. Her voice warbles … because, obvi, she's water right now.

"Unde-e-e-e-r my foot."

I have no idea what the heck that means, but I glance down. I see a tiny green armored horse trying to swim through the water in Becca's foot. But she keeps moving her foot so he can't get away.

I scoop up Hopper and hold on tight, so the squirmy little guy can't escape.

Becca says, "Clothes," and then sloshes off to go find herself something to change into, because, despite the fact that she's made of water, her clothes still burnt to a crisp in that fire.

As did the clothing of the trolls I turn back to eye. Dang. I didn't notice at first because they were basically charred. But, yup. Nudity. All around.

Tar got the worst of the burns, by far. If Bennett hadn't been here, the troll might actually have been hurt. His smooth yellow skin is so burnt that it's not just black, it's white in places. Ashy. Tar gnashes his teeth in fury. But, unlike the fighting trolls, he's smart enough to remain silent as Flowers and Petey make their way over.

Flowers says, "Good thing Bennett was here and contained that dragon thire. Otherwise, you mightta been toast, Tar." Flowers just totally goes with his lisp as he stares half-heartedly around the club, as if looking for suspects. But everyone's cleared out.

The gangster glares down at Flowers. "Gonna investigate, you son of a rock?"

Flowers shows his teeth.

But I don't have time for male posturing. I'm still reeling. *Dragon fire?!* Someone attacked us all with dragon fire? Ohhh. My heart squeezes tight. If Bennett hadn't been here … I'd be a pile of ash on the ground.

I glance around the club. But the fire was only in our little area. The ceiling above us is a gaping hole to the starlight. The flames were so hot, they melted the metal back and shot up to the sky.

This was a targeted hit. And Tar got the worst of it. Who did it? I glance down at the little armored horse that's wriggling in my hands. Did Hopper do it to get away? Did he somehow find that secret passage and figure that dragon fire was another thing he could use or sell? He seems like he's slimy enough to do something like that. A guy who chains up a girlfriend and leaves her for days …

My hand tightens around him and I can't help the anger in my tone as I glare down at the miniature shifter and say, "You're under arrest."

I watch Flowers and Becca effectively melt Hopper down in questioning. It's either because they're super amazing investigators or because they threaten to drop him off back at the Tar Pit with those angry juiced up trolls if he lies.

Hopper admits to stealing Rachel's urine, chaining her up, and leaving her so he could sell it. He admits he had an ongoing deal with Louise to drain a bit of Frank's blood sweat.

"She was giving me free hits, man. How could I pass that up?"

"You couldn't," Flowers shrugged. "Until you decided to take Louise outta the picture."

"What?"

"Why'd you kill her?"

"Louise was my hook up! Why would I kill her?"

Becca shrugs. "Didn't seem like you needed her when you approached those trolls."

"Yeah, because, clearly, I'm a total expert. I shoulda' never trusted Rachel. She doesn't know shit. Marian's the whole brains of that operation—"

I lean forward in my seat. "Marian?"

"Yeah. Rachel didn't tell me her pee wasn't worth shit," Hopper says this bitterly, as if Rachel deliberately misled him into chaining her up.

"Who's Marian?" I press.

"Rachel's best friend."

"More details please." I swear, all the Nappies have made this guy slow. Or maybe it's the giant goose-egg from when I flicked his grasshorse head with my finger as we climbed into the van to come back here.

"They grew up together. I dunno. Marian's boring. Straight edge. She's like ... the smart one." He blinks, hard, and holds his head in his hands. "I'm dizzy. Don't you think I should get checked out? I mean, you sent all those trolls to the hospital after the dragon fire."

"Speaking of dragon fire, how'd you smuggle it in?" I ask.

"WHAT? You think I'm crazy enough to touch that stuff? *Hell no.*"

I really want to punch Hopper right now.

But Flowers shocks me out of my ire when he shrugs and says, "I know you didn't bring the dragon thire."

"You do?" Hopper and I ask in stereo.

"Your clothes slipped to the ground when you shi … turned into your animal. They weren't burnt. No vials of anything other than pee in there."

If Hopper didn't throw fire at us … who did?

Becca and I exchange a glance. She doesn't look like she knows either. When I glance at Flowers, he shrugs. Great. Another unanswered question in this case. A dangerous one. Because someone out there is willing to steal dragon fire and use it.

Hopper starts coughing. At first, I think he's just putting us on, but after a minute, he starts to wheeze.

I turn to Flowers. "I think this guy might actually need medical attention."

Flowers' nostrils flare as if I've done something annoying. But Hopper might have a concussion. Has definitely inhaled smoke. And his answers are useless. He's given us some of what we wanted. But still … I agree with him. He never had a reason to kill Louise. He benefitted from his arrangement with her, sick as it was.

"I guess," Flowers sighs.

We arrive at the hospital and let the nurses get to work examining Hopper. One of them clucks over the bump on his forehead. She walks away and comes back with a goose. She lays Hopper down and plops the goose right on top of his head.

"It'll heal faster this way," she reassures us.

I hold in a snort as I exchange a glance with Becca. But then yellow goo starts dripping down Hopper's face and when the nurse lifts off the goose—sure enough, the swelling is gone. Hopper's goose egg has cracked. The nurse hums as she swipes at the ooze and mops up the yolk.

I shake my head, glad for the zillionth time that I do not work in medicine.

When that nurse leaves and another comes in, Flowers pulls the new one aside. "We need to ask a doc about spell reversal."

The nurse—a dodore with a single eye, a single leg, and red hair—eyes Flowers. "You try one of them male enhancement spells?" she asks tiredly.

"What? No!" Flowers jerks his head at me. "She put a spell on me so I can't say the letter ..."

Clearly, he can't finish his sentence, so I roll my eyes and step in. "I accidentally made him unable to say the letter 'f.'"

The nurse sighs. "Seventh floor."

I perk up a bit. "So, reversal is easy? I also accidentally turned my boyfriend's hand into catnip."

The nurse shakes her head, her single eye disapproving, as she says, "Maybe you'd be better off not using spells."

"Agreed," Flowers glares at me.

But I ignore him. "Becca, you good with Hopper?"

She nods.

I pull out my phone and text Luke. "Sweet. Let's go get this dopey magic of mine all reversed."

We hit the seventh floor and a skinny minotaur doc in a lab coat immediately approaches us. He snorts when he reaches Flowers, then covers his mouth.

"Sorry, you a cat shifter of some kind?"

"Tiger," Flowers responds.

"One sec, I'll get my colleague over. I'm allergic. Sorry." The guy walks off, tail swishing, and full on sneezes.

Flowers grumbles. "It's not like I'm a tiger now."

I shrug and say, "But you probably have cat hair all over the place, right? Doesn't that stuff get caught in, like, crevices?"

Flowers just glares. But, whatever. That's basically his normal face to me at this point. I stare at the wall until my phone buzzes.

I'm here.

Luke's text sends giddiness right through me as I text him back and tell him where to meet us.

By the time he arrives, the allergic minotaur has been replaced by a tense, fifty-something valkyrie with grey hair and a harsh booming voice.

"You're not dying. Why're you on my floor?" she booms.

"Well, my magic is a little funky and—" I cut off my sentence when I notice Flowers has gone to his knees behind me and is shoving Luke's hand on his face.

"Stop that!" I smack Flowers away. "Control yourself. Geez!"

Flowers just snarls at me and his tiger nose and whiskers spring up on his face.

"Catnip hand," the valkyrie sighs as I try and separate the guys.

"Yup," Luke agrees, trying to hold his hand out of Flowers' grip.

Flowers does not appreciate our attempts to minimize his addiction. His fangs elongate and he snaps at my hand when I try to grab him by the waist and drag him away from Luke.

"Please!" I look up at the lady doc. "Help!"

"Unless you want me to strike him down dead and send him to Valhalla, you needa' tell me what's wrong so I can get him some meds. He an addict?"

"NO!" I have to shove Flowers back with my whole body.

Luke takes a few steps back and grabs a blanket off a patient bed to wrap his hand and staunch the catnip smell. "Lyon has the unusual magic to make people lose things. She accidentally made her boss there lose the ability to say the letter F. We tried to lose something of mine and then reverse the spell but um... the equation obviously didn't work out. Her boss must be part of the fifty percent of cats that's very affected by nip." He waves his catnip green hand. Flowers' head swivels to keep the catnip in sight at all times.

The valkyrie huffs and walks off without another word.

"Is she helping us?" I ask.

But Luke doesn't get a chance to respond. Because Flowers tackles him to the ground and starts licking and biting at the blanket around Luke's hand.

"You dingleberry! Get off my boyfriend!" I try to yank Flowers away. Here's the thing though. Flowers is strong.

When he lets one of his hands shift to a tiger paw, he's strong with claws. Not a good combo when his opponent is helpless little ole me.

Luke grabs me and suddenly, we're across the room with superspeed. But we don't get to rest for a second before Flowers is leaping right at us like a wild animal.

"Walloping whiskers! His eyes have shifted!" I cry.

Luke sweeps me up in his arms and races like the wind to another corner. Then another. I start to get dizzy when he gets to the third corner.

"STOP!" the valkyrie returns and yells at us, spreading her wings and smacking Flowers down mid-leap.

His head hits the floor. And I feel slightly bad as he stands up, dizzy and grasping at his poor skull.

"You, come here," the valkyrie snaps at Luke.

I vaguely realize that she's never bothered to introduce herself. I glance at her nametag. Brynhildr. Figures. Brynhildr sounds like a bitter bitch name.

"Stick your hand in this," Brynhildr commands, pouring out a smelly jar of yellow liquid into a bowl.

"What is it—"

Brynhildr cuts Luke off and shoves his hand into the bowl, blanket and all. She lets the stuff absorb for a minute before pulling his hand out and peeling the shredded bits of blanket back to reveal a very normal-looking vamp hand.

"It worked," I breathe. "What is that magical stuff?"

"Biofluid," she answers stiffly, turning to Flowers, who's straightening up.

His limbs have all returned to human and he scratches his cheek as the last of his whiskers disappears. He nods toward the bowl of yellow liquid. "That work on me?"

Brynhildr gives a nod.

Flowers dips his hand into the bowl and swipes it across his throat. "Shit! This gunk stinks."

Brynhildr furrows her brows. "What are you doing?"

Flowers stares at her. "I thought you said this stu--, this goo would get rid o- my talking issue."

"Your issue is on your vocal cords, not on your skin," Brynhildr replies.

Flowers mouth drops open. "No. You can't be serious."

"Yup."

She takes her yellow pitcher and pours some of it into a cup. "You need to drink it."

Flowers takes the cup and sniffs it warily. "What is it again?"

"I already told you. Biofluid."

And that's when my hand betrays me. It flies to my mouth as I realize what she's saying. My eyes widen and a stupid, stupid loud gulp runs through my throat.

Flowers glances over. It only takes half a second for him to look at my expression before he realizes what it means. "This is mixed shithter pee, isn't it?"

21

"Y ou have to drink it, too!" Flowers argues.

"No, I don't!"

"This is your thault!"

"You ran in on me when I was changing!"

"What?" Luke interjects, coming to stand between me and Flowers and crossing his arms in a very pissed-off, protective boyfriend way.

"That's sweet, but like, he didn't mean to," I touch Luke's non-pee arm. "He was chasing a suspect."

"Yeah, so you gotta drink it." Flowers reiterates.

"That's not logical."

"You're gonna drink it or you will end up cleaning the men's bathroom for the next year!"

"You can't—"

"On every thloor."

I clench my fists. "Fine!" I snarl.

"Good," Flowers snarls right back.

Brynhildr just rolls her eyes and pours another cup of pee.

Luke takes my hand. "You don't have to do this, you know?"

"You'll still date me?" I ask.

"After you mouthwash like eighty times," he rolls his eyes.

I let out a deep breath. "Fair enough." I glare around Luke at Flowers. "At least some people can be mature."

"Thuck you," Flowers says.

Just as he's embracing his lisp, we're gonna be rid of it.

Brynhildr hands me my cup of Magic Eraser.

I check with her. "This is really the only cure?"

"Only one in this realm."

I take the cup but make a face as I slink back behind Luke. The cup is warm. Ew.

Flowers stomps over to stand where he can see me.

Tiger butt hair. There goes my plan to tilt my cup a bit and just get him to drink it. We glare at one another and raise our hands slowly, like cowboys about to pull their weapons.

"On three," Flowers says.

Our hands slowly creep upward. My stomach's already churning in anticipation and disgust. I can't believe my life has come to this.

The edge of the cup reaches my lips as Flowers' mutters, "Three."

I close my eyes. But I can't do it. I cannot willingly make myself drink urine.

I crack my eyelid and glance at Flowers.

"You were supposed to drink it," he growls, still holding a full cup.

My eyes fly open. "So were you!"

There's a feminine throat clearing noise behind me. I turn to see Becca standing in the door. "Is this a bad time to say that those of us who've been working have actually found a new lead? Hopper pointed us toward another suspect."

Flowers and I both lower our cups of 'biofluid.'

Becca arches a brow haughtily as she continues, "He saw a cat-peacock at Louise's that night. Says it's Rachel's best friend. Bill's girlfriend."

Flowers grumbles, "We never interviewed a cat-peacock."

Becca says, "Well, looks like we need to talk to Rachel again."

"She still at the jail?"

"Just bonded out," Becca responds. "Which means, if she knows anything about what happened … she's probably heading straight for her friend to warn her to book it."

Flowers sets down his cup and bolts for the stairs. Guess he's more interested in solving this case than curing his lisp.

Brynhildr hands me a screw on lid for my cup. "Trust me, that guy's gonna want it."

"I'm not sure he will." I really don't want to carry around a cup of pee.

The valkyrie shakes her head and rolls her eyes. "Men are always changing their minds. When they're at home, they're always wishing they were in battle. When they're actually in battle? They whine about going home." She pushes the cup toward me. "When no one's around, that guy'll come to his senses and drink it. Cat shifters are stubborn and prideful. Maybe try mixing it with a little milk."

I chew my lip, but Luke takes the cup out of my hands and sighs. "I really don't want to join you in the men's restrooms for the next year, gorgeous. So, I'll put this in the fridge at your place for you."

I sigh. "I guess that's alright."

Becca looks at me then back at Luke. "I'm gonna tell the boss you tried a sip of that and yakked. Have a good morning, kids." She winks and then skips to the steps to follow Flowers.

I turn to Luke and grin. "Guess I'm getting off work early. Whatcha' wanna do?"

He smiles down at me and grabs my hand with his pee-free one. "Let's go see what kind of demon you are."

I groan. "We all know it's gonna be a slothy one."

"No, we don't."

"Yes, we do," I argue childishly as we step onto an elevator and press the button for Doctor Eduardo's floor. "Because that's the only logical choice."

Luke blows a raspberry at my logic.

I laugh. "I love that you're so hot, but such a nerd. How the hell did that happen?"

Luke smiles down at me. "We talked about this, didn't we?"

"About what?"

"I've told you about my life when I was a human, right?"

I shake my head.

"I could have sworn …" Luke shakes his head and grins. "Must be because it feels like I've told you everything." He leans back against the wall of the elevator and tucks me into the crook of his arm.

I snuggle in, enjoying the feel of him and the crisp, clean scent of his shirt.

"When I was a kid, I got sick. Polio."

My ribs stab my heart. I freeze.

Luke doesn't notice. He keeps talking. "I ended up in a wheelchair. It's why I like 'nerdy' things, I guess. It's also why … even though Cookie's—different—she's so important to me. When she changed me, she kinda gave me my life back."

The elevator dings and the doors open. Luke stands up and moves toward the door. But I'm frozen.

Fuck.

Fuck.

Fuck.

I'm a smear on the pavement. I'm not just dead. I'm obliterated.

Luke tugs me again and I move forward, but my head's in a fog. We're at Doctor Eduardo's desk before I know it. And he's handing over a paper. But I'm just standing there with it in my hand like a dummy. My neck feels hot. It's burning up. But my hands are icy. The world is wrong, wrong, wrong.

How could this happen? The perfect guy. The perfect vamp. And one sip from me could end him.

I have to tell him.

"Ly, are you okay?" Luke's bending his knees, holding my shoulders, staring into my eyes.

I try to focus on him.

"Hey, don't be nervous, okay?" he rubs little circles onto my back. "It'll be fine." Then he frowns. "Was it what I told you? Did I do something wrong?"

I shake my head. He didn't do anything wrong. He's not wrong. He's perfect. I'm wrong. Me. I'm the problem.

"Do you want me to read it?" he gestures at the paper in my hands.

I nod. Yes. He should read it. Maybe if we break eye contact for a second, I'll actually be able to think. I'll actually be able to force myself to say what I need to say. I'll be able to tell him that I'm the reason his ex, Georgina died. Someone knocked me out and tempted her with my blood. My blood turns vamps human. She was turned human and killed. I'll be able to tell him about Alec, my high school vamp boyfriend … and how I didn't know that my blood was poisonous to vamps. I'll be able to say I'm no good for him. And that this relationship—the most perfect thing in my entire life—needs to end.

I take a deep, gasping breath as Luke unfolds the paper. But before I can turn the whirlwind inside my lungs into words, Luke drops the paper to the floor.

He takes a step back, away from me. He sets my cup of urine on the table. My eyes meet his and my own misery is reflected back at me.

"I ... need to think."

Then he's gone, vampire speed leaving nothing but wind in his wake.

22

J R wraps me in her afghan. She steers me toward a huge six-foot-wide pink flower and forces its petals to open into a semi-recliner. I sink into the plant, ignoring how the side of my face gets coated in pollen.

Tears track down my cheeks.

JR tries to sit on the ground next to me, but she has to move some kind of spiky plant out of the way. She coos at it like it was a baby as she carries it to a spot near a window.

Even through my heartbreak, I find the strength to roll my eyes at her plant-coddling. "Actual person here. With actual problems."

JR points a finger at me. "Don't start missy. Plants have feelings, too."

"Do their feelings include black-as-death heartbreak?"

"Maybe."

"Well, they can't talk about them, so get over here and let me cry on your shoulder!" I pout.

"You make best-friending sound so appealing," JR comments as she grabs the wine and two glasses.

I bury my face in my hands. "I just—I shouldn't be this upset. Why am I this upset? We barely started dating." I kick my feet out further on the far petal and scooch down until I'm staring at the ceiling. It's that awful popcorn texture.

JR comes over and puts the bottle and two full glasses near me. Then she lifts my feet, takes a seat, and puts my feet right back down on her lap. "Talk to me, Ly-Ly."

I stare at the ceiling, listless. Disbelieving. I hand her my test results, which have been crumpled in my hand since the Broomer dropped me off here.

She scans the read out. "Succubus? Are you joking?"

I shake my head and laugh bitterly, reaching for my wine.

"What rank is that?" she asks. (I'd texted her about demon rankings after my bathroom meet up with Nicolette.) "I totally thought you were gluttony."

"Third."

"Third! That's high. Crud!"

I nod and then down most of the sweet, bubbly glass of white Riesling in half a second. "I wish I was joking. But Doctor Eduardo came over and told me that my leg turns chicken because I'm a direct descendent of Asphodel—the original lust demon."

"No!" JR stands and my feet fall out of her lap and grabs her phone. She does a quick internet search.

She turns and shows me a picture of a hot-as-sin demon with black hair, an eyebrow piercing, tattoos covering his neck and chest, red horns that fade to gold at the tips protruding from his forehead. He's so hot he's hard to look at, until you scan down to see one very obvious rooster leg. His pants have been cut off to showcase it. There are two female demons fawning all over him in the picture.

"Damn. Your great grand-dad or whatever, is hot!"

I curl my lip and pour myself a second glass of wine. I don't care about headaches tomorrow. The heartache today is worse. "Don't be gross. And focus on my misery here, please. I don't want to be a lust demon. I want to be a slothy lazybutt demon. I want to be a useless demon. I want to be lower ranked than Luke."

JR sits back down on the edge of the petal facing me. "But dude. Succubus. That means you're sexy and sassy and stuff!" JR slaps my leg. "Why is that such a bad thing?"

I sigh, throwing my arm over my forehead as I picture Luke's face. The shock, the disappointment. It sprinkles all kind of sadness through me. And that sadness clings and shines like glitter. I can't seem to shake it. "I think it's why I turned Alec back in high school. My blood has a little succubus in it and they're a higher-ranking demon than vamps."

"Lost." JR massages my foot. "Why the heck would demon rank matter?"

"I forgot to tell you about that part. Didn't think it was relevant. Nicolette said demons aren't allowed to attack those of higher rank. Maintains order in hell or something."

"But … you *let* Alec bite you back in the day. It wasn't an attack."

I groan. "Don't remind me. Besides, obviously, I know it wasn't an attack. But my dumb blood doesn't seem to know the difference."

JR yanks on my foot. "Luke would never attack you. Or bite you if you told him not to."

I glance up at her and shake my head, smacking my cheeks against the headrest. "Accidents happen though. And I couldn't live with myself … turning him human is …" my voice cracks, "a deal breaker."

"He said that?"

I shake my head. I don't want to talk about it anymore. It sucks. Demonology sucks. I take another big drink and snuggle further into the flower, wishing it had pillows. I see my purse on the floor. It shakes slightly as my phone buzzes. Someone must be calling.

I ignore the call and stare into my glass, letting JR's comforting words gloss over me. They're nice words, like "You're perfect … he's lucky to have you …" and things like that. But I don't really listen. I just kind of exist.

Until that damn buzzing starts again.

"Ugh," I grumble as I lean over and grab my purse roughly. I pull out my phone and turn it over to see four missed calls.

I unlock my phone and see three missed calls from Becca and one missed call from Luke. I also have several texts.

Becca's texts say— *Rachel slipped us. Apparently, she can fly. Ideas?*

There's also a text from Luke: *You aren't home. Please call me.*

Call him so he can break up with me on the phone (not via text) like a gentleman? No thanks.

But then a picture pops up. A text from Sarah. She, Tabby, and Luke are sitting together in her living room. He looks stiff and highly uncomfortable. Great. No way he's getting to leave until we've seen each other.

Son of a tiger. Why do those women have to be so interfering? I blow out a breath. "I gotta go."

"Why?"

I hold up the pic of Luke with Tabby and Sarah.

"Oh, send that to me."

"Why?"

She shrugs. "Dartboard face for later."

I roll my eyes but send it. "He's not a dartboard face."

"All guys are dartboard faces eventually."

I laugh and she saves the photo to her pics. "Ew! I don't know why I saved this one!" she exclaims.

"What?" I ask.

She holds up her phone and shows me the pic I sent of that nasty sink over at Louise's. The sink is ringed in green … I squint. The entire sink is ringed in wet, green feathers. I'd written it off as grime, but looking now, it's definitely feathers. Like peacock feathers.

My mind flashes back to bathroom and the open window. A window that wasn't big enough for any animal bigger than a cat to fit through.

The cat-peacock was there that night. Hopper's telling the truth. Rachel's best friend. Bill's girlfriend. What did Hopper call her? Straight edge. No drugs. She must have been pissed at Louise for getting Bill hooked. Pissed when he went over there and never came back.

My mind races as it replays the possibilities. Rachel and her BFF went to the nap shack searching for answers about Bill. Maybe her BFF could smell something was off. I don't know enough about cat noses to be sure. Maybe she could scent Bill's body. She was pissed at Louise but hid it. Maybe even shifted into a cat and acted like she was gonna cooperate.

Yeah, that theory's a good one. I can see it all happening in my head.

She was a cat peacock. Mostly cat. Louise poured her the milk. She drank it. Maybe a baby started fussing and Louise stepped away. Could Bill's girlfriend have gotten into the secret passage and found his body? The opening dropped into the kitchen. Maybe if she had peacock wings … Maybe she flew up and found Bill's body. Maybe she took his fire. Thought about using it on Louise.

But there were so many babies there. Maybe she didn't want to hurt them? I'm not sure. But it would make me hesitate.

She's the smart one. That's what Hopper said. She knows hexes. She flew back down to the kitchen … shifted, wrote out the hex on the knife, and shifted back.

Louise came back. But then Flowers was at the door.

She heard the word, "Police," and the cat peacock ran to hide … in the bathroom.

There was all that blue hair that coated my uniform …

I sit straight up and slop wine all over myself.

"What the—"JR starts.

But I hold up a hand and dial Becca. "I know who did it."

23

I rush to the dry cleaners, blood pumping so hard it sounds like the base beat of a song in my ears as I run. I should've put it together sooner.

Louise doped William Henson on the regular. Who knows if she'd been stealing bits of flame on the regular. But then he overdosed. And she hid him. Like trash.

He might not have had a dragon clan to avenge him anymore. But that didn't mean he didn't have family.

Sometimes, your family is made up of people you choose. People who bond with you when times are hard. Like Jacob and I after I lost my dad. Sometimes, your adopted family is made up of friends who see the world the way that you do, laugh at your crappy jokes, and support you even when you abandon them to deal with Arnold the werewolf alone because you're pursuing a dream you never even knew you had. JR's family to me. Sometimes, your family is made up of people who've been so important in your past, that they will always be part of your inner circle no matter what—that's Bennett for me.

We've spent all this time thinking that Bill was used by Louise, without anyone to defend him. But what if that's not true? I'm betting that's not true.

Becca said it best. Women be vengeful bitches. If his girlfriend was a straight edge, she might have attacked Louise and her boss, Tar. His girlfriend might have stood up for him against the people responsible for his death even after he was gone.

I yank open the door to Sue's Cleaners and find I'm the first there.

There's no one at the counter. "Sandpaper tiger tongues!" I mutter under my breath as the door swings shut and the bell tinkles behind me.

A pretty brunette in her mid-thirties pops her head around the corner. She gives me a big, bright fuchsia lipstick smile. "One sec!" she calls.

I blink. I'm not sure, but her neck looks an awful lot like Rachel's did at the station. Too long for her body. Like a giraffe shifter neck.

I don't have time to process before Flowers and Bennett have rushed into the front room and crowd me.

"Where is she?" Flowers snarls, just as the busty brunette walks over in her starched black collared shirt.

The woman sighs as I read her nametag. This is the illustrious Sue. She must be the owner. "Did Marian give you a hard time about a stiffening spell?" she asks Flowers wearily. She says, "I've told that girl a million times— MARIAN!" Sue yells as if Marian's in the back. Here.

If she's here, Rachel must not have gotten here yet. Rachel must not have warned her yet. Marian must not know we know. But my eyes recall her face when she saw the hair on my uniform.

She knew we were investigating Louise's death. And she burnt the evidence. Unluckily for Marian, I take photos of nearly everything.

I stare at the back wall—as if that will make Marian materialize—while Flowers argues with Sue.

"I'm not here about a stithening spell!" Flowers lisps.

Sue stares him up and down skeptically, pursing her bright lips. "You sure?"

Flowers must be beyond pissed, because his eyes start to go tiger. His pupils get round and his irises change from brown to yellow.

So do Sue's. And then, she starts to growl.

The alpha predator tension shoots through the roof and my pulse instantly spikes. My body says, "Run!!!!!"

This is bad. Sue's a tiger? I thought she was a giraffe … maybe she's a combo. Everyone else on this damn case is. A giraffe and a tiger. A Girger. But there's no telling what parts of her shift to what. What if she's got tiger teeth? Claws?

Flowers growls louder than Sue did, and he takes a step closer to her. Their eyes stay locked.

I grab Bennett's arm and look up at him. "What do we do?"

Bennett doesn't answer. He grins and pulls my hand off his arm. Then he leaps over the counter past Sue.

She turns, but Flowers tackles her and pins her to the ground. "You're under arrest for growling at an officer."

"That's a bogus charge." Her neck starts to elongate and get stripes. I was right. Girger.

When I'm sure Flowers has her pinned, I use the latch to let myself through the half door to the other side of the counter.

Flowers has let his fangs come out and he's showing them to Sue, who's struggling beneath him.

I carefully hug the wall as I round the two wrestling shifters.

I make it to the back where there are baskets and baskets full of smelly unwashed clothes. There's even a basket with clothes that glow like my uniform did. It's labeled "Zombified. Handle with Care. Brain Cycle Only."

I find Bennett standing across a table from Marian. It looks like he's whispering to her.

As soon as Marian sees me, however, she must put the pieces together. She must know we're here for her. Her eyes widen, and her piercings glint as she turns and bolts away.

"Cat-shredded couches!" I hiss as I run after her.

She goes into a forest of hanging clothes. There are vamp capes floating midair under ultraviolet lights. There are fairy wings hung on a line like laundry. My hand brushes one and it's like a sticky spiderweb.

Marian yanks open a door and disappears into a second room. I follow.

Here are the hexes. I can see all kinds of troll clothes, glowing with bright yellow troll blood. On the edges of the clothing, small equations wiggle like worms, slowly eating up the stains.

I wonder if Sue's Cleaners takes in illegal troll fight clothes as I zip through the room, trying to follow the flying blue mane that's Marian's hair.

She whips around another corner. I follow, breathing hard, wondering if Bennett had to stop to help Flowers. WTF is taking him so long?

Another room. This time, the clothes seem more human. Wizard clothes. There's a burnt smell that emanates from these clothes. Maybe they're from the local high school. Uniforms or something. I shove aside heavy cloaks and try to keep my eyes on her feet in front of me, because that's all I can see with these racks in the way. Then the racks jolt and start moving. Someone's flipped a switch or said a spell to get the racks rotating; the clothes whip past me, sleeves whirling out from the speed. I go forward but the clothes press against me hard and and fast, shoving me sideways; I can't push through. I have to drop to the floor and scoot along on my stomach to chase our perp.

Of course, Marian doesn't care about breaking laws at this point. Marian fully shifts in public. Her clothes shred and fall to the ground as her body changes. While she's mostly a gorgeous jewel-blue cat, her blue fur transitions to feathers near her rear and she sports luxurious green tail feathers complete with eyes that would make any peacock proud.

I'd be lying if I didn't say I wasn't completely dazed for a second. Cat peacocks ... peacats are so beautiful that they should be a thing. Everywhere. There should have been an ancient religion for them.

Marian's cat speed lets her slink away even faster, and as I pass the last of the clothing racks (Bennett starts crawling along behind me—I can hear him muttering), Marian leaps onto the top of the huge industrial washing machines in the back. She leaps from one to the next.

"Stop, you're under arrest!" I yell. "For the murder of Louise Grant!"

Does that stop her? *Psh!* Did you really think it would?

She leaps onto a pipe that runs the length of the ceiling and army crawls toward a small window that's open near the ceiling.

I look around for something to throw on her—a blanket or something—I latch onto a witch's black gown and throw it. It lands on Marian's tail but doesn't stop her progress.

I bite my lip. I don't want to make her lose her footing, but I have to stop her before she gets out of here.

I don't want to use my power, but it seems like I have no choice.

"You've lost your cat shifter abilities!" I yell. My leg burns.

Marian's fur wavers and turns into feathers. Her head grows smaller and her neck lengthens. Her front paws turn into wings. Her back paws grow skinny and scaled until they become claws.

She transforms into a full peacock. Her neck swivels and she stares at me for a second, blinking. I'm not sure if she's more shocked or more pissed. Probably some version of both.

Her claws slip on the pipe and she slides sideways. For a second, it looks like she might tumble backward. But then she spreads her wings and bursts into flight.

But then my magic wavers. I feel it shake inside my stomach as Marian flies back up to the pole. She barely has time to land before she's a cat again.

"What the three-legged tiger?" I gasp. My leg fades from chicken to human faster than normal. "You've lost your cat shifter abilities!" I call out again, as Marian slinks along the pole.

But she doesn't shift again. She just throws a disdainful glance back at me before she heads for the window.

My stupid freaking powers! What's wrong with them?

I grab a suit coat and toss it at her next, nailing her in the back. She tumbles to the floor; her cat balance ensures she lands on her feet. I run forward to grab her, reaching for my handcuffs—but suddenly Bennett's tripping to a stop beside me. I hear a *thunk* as a huge container tips over next to me. Then whirl of dust settles on my skin.

My limbs get as hard as rocks.

I swivel my neck to see the barrel and Bennett. He's locked in place, white powder up to his calves. The barrel beside him reads: *"Stiffening Powder. Dissolve 1:10 for solution."*

Shit!

My limbs lock from my feet to my hips. I can't move. I feel the magic spread upward to my torso. I turn my neck to look at Marian but I can't do anything but watch as she shifts into a naked human, her back covered in a gorgeous dragon tattoo, the letters 'EWNM' woven into the dragon's wings. I can't do anything but watch as she runs out the back door.

24

"Yowling stiffening solution!" I curse and rub my stiff limbs yet again. It's taken over an hour for them to come back to life and the fallen-asleep prickling sensation is awful. It's as bad as a bite from a daggle (a witch's dog enchanted to give painful burning bites).

Flowers eventually realized Bennett and I didn't come back and went to check on us. He'd let Sue off with a warning about her growl, then supervised the swarm of cops that searched Sue's Cleaners and spread out through the neighborhood looking for Marian. He also got pretty happy over intercepting Rachel, who ran up just as the search party started.

Rachel is, once again, in custody for questioning. She's lucky she got here late, or Flowers definitely would have tried to slap her with accessory after the fact charges, too.

I've had to watch everything from afar as Bennett and I have been stuck here on the back of an ambulance, getting treated for exposure to magical stiffening chemicals by two dwarves with more attitude than medical knowledge.

"Great furry night," I groan as my neck cracks. "Lost our perp, broke up, got stiffened—no idea why anyone would do *that* on purpose—"

"On the other hand, you've perthected the art of complaining," Flowers interjects.

I just glare at him. "Love the lisp."

His eyes narrow to slits. "Your fault."

I shake my head. "Not anymore. You could have fixed it."

Bennett interjects, "Broke up?"

I stare at his brilliant green eyes and shake my head. "Apparently, I'm part succubus."

Ben's eyes widen because he immediately knows what it means for me and vamps.

Flowers starts to ask but he's interrupted by Darrell, who's found what he thinks might be a peacock feather. Flowers stomps off after the mummy to go identify it.

Ben stares at me for a while and there's a long awkward moment, before I say, "What were you telling Marian when I got in there?"

Bennett's face flushes. "I … just let her know we'd found Bill."

"She'd have seen that online. Or in the paper." Something's off.

He swallows and glances away from me. "I just—"

The pieces fall together in my head as I shake my hand and try and get the feeling back. I stand, suddenly unable to be around Bennett. What the hell? He didn't trip. He didn't knock over that stiffening solution on accident. He let Marian get away.

The revelation knocks me off balance. I feel dizzy. I mean, Bennett's my boss. Plus … he's him. He's supposed to be one of the good guys.

"Imma go home and pass out. See you tomorrow, Boss." I try the avoidance technique. Because I'm seriously at a loss here.

Bennett's face falls a bit. "Sure. See ya. Sorry again about …"

But the trailing off does it. Somehow it sets me off. Maybe I would have snapped and said something anyway, because I'm me. But apologizing? He knows what he did. He knows it's wrong. I turn back and stare Bennett in the eye. "Be careful. When you cross lines, they start to look grey. And then they aren't lines anymore."

His gaze hardens and his nostrils flare.

I shake my head. I can't. I just can't.

I turn and limp home. In the distance, behind me, I hear shouts and squawking. They've caught her.

Unlike with prior cases, I don't feel any sense of victory that we've nabbed the killer. Marian offed a selfish, ruthless old hag. A little part of me sympathizes with Bennett.

I hope Marian gets off with a light sentence. I'm sure she will, since technically what I've got to pin her to the scene is a photo. Unless, of course, one of the zillion hair samples tie her there. But ... who knows?

My mind starts to wander away from the case and back to more pressing issues. Like Luke.

My hands get clammy as I see the lights in the distance for my little fourplex. My phone buzzes again in my purse, but when I check it, it's my mother, so I ignore the call.

I get closer and see Sarah's curtains are open and clearly, they're watching for me.

My tongue sticks to the roof of my mouth and I shuffle closer.

When I'm about ten feet from the door, it comes flying open. And suddenly, two strong arms are around me, sweeping me up into a hug.

"Hey! You didn't call me," Luke scolds.

Wait. What? He's hugging me? Failure to compute.

"I ... uh ..."

"Flowers give you a bad time?"

"We ... tracked down our suspect. Had to chase them."

Luke pulls back and looks me over, head to toe. "Are you okay?"

My mouth opens and closes a couple times. Did someone erase his memory? Did I have a hallucination at the hospital?

"I'm sorry. I thought we broke up."

"WHAT?" Luke exclaims.

"WHAT?" Tabby and Sarah say from the doorway.

I blink dumbly. Luke scoops me into his arms and carries me up the stairs. He finds my key in my purse and unlocks the door, letting me down once we're in the relative privacy of my apartment.

"They're just gonna watch on the crystal ball," I say absently, imagining Tabby plonking her ball down on Sarah's dining table.

Luke feels my face with his hands, like he's checking me for a fever. "Are you feeling okay, Ly?"

I shake my head. Because I'm not alright. Not at all. "At the hospital. You saw my results. And you ran."

Luke runs a hand down his face. He looks devastated. "Ly, I'm so soo sorry. That had nothing to do—well, I mean it had to do with your results. But it had more to do with my mother."

"What?" I let myself fall into my purple couch, my hips still a little stiff from the powder. I sit back in the soft cushions and run my hands over the velvet plush. What is going on? What's he saying?

"She's been so pushy about you. Asking questions. Nudging us along. She even asked if I was gonna bite you."

I wrinkle my brow.

"You don't ask about biting, Ly. That's like asking me about my jerk off habits."

"Okay."

Luke blows out a breath and sits in my armchair. "I think my mom wants me to turn human."

"WHAT?" I pop up in the couch and stare at him. "Why? Why the hell would she want that?"

He shakes his head. "A million reasons. I'm an embarrassment. Or a burden. Or she wants to turn me again but have me so indebted that this time I can't back away from her business …"

I'm up and then sitting on his lap in two seconds, hugging him as hard as I can. "That's awful!" I stroke my hand down his hair.

He bites his lip and studies my eyes. "I swear. I'm sorry. What happened at the hospital … I freaked out when I saw those results. I've been wondering why she was so pushy. I didn't want to scare you when I talked about her. But she knows. She knows. When I saw your results it just clicked. I didn't mean to—"

I cover his lips with a finger. "It's okay."

"It's not."

"Well, it sucks. But you'll make it up to me."

He nods. "I will. I promise I will."

I grin and lean in to give him a soft chaste kiss. Even that sends my stomach spiraling in happiness. I can't help the smile that bursts onto my face when I lean back and stare up at his gorgeous blue eyes. "I'm so glad we're not broken up."

"Me too."

"I promise I won't make you human. I won't use my succubusness or whatever on you. I like you just the way you are."

"I promise I won't run like that again."

"I promise I'll call you back next time you text." I snuggle into Luke's chest, tracing one of the tattoos on his forearm.

"I promise … not to drag you into any more shit with Cookie. I'm done with her."

"What do you mean?" I glance up.

"I mean … I filed that emancipation scroll you gave me."

My stomach drops. I lean back and stare up at Luke's face. He looks just as serious as I feel. Shit's about to get real. "She's gonna be pissed," I warn.

He shrugs, "What's she gonna do about it? I've got a badass girlfriend who's a succubus. If she attacks, you could turn her human. She better watch her back."

I laugh and settle back against his chest, though we both know I'm no match for Cookie. "Stay here today?" I ask.

"I'll stay here any day you want me."

"Well, I'd better get you a toothbrush then, because I'm gonna want you every day."

"Fine by me."

And even though Cookie's wrath looms like some distant storm cloud, even though Bennett's choice tonight has me questioning our tentative friendship, none of that can touch me. Because I'm in Luke's arms.

WE MUST HAVE FALLEN ASLEEP ON MY COUCH. DAMMIT. My
neck hurts. I peer around my living room, eyelashes half
cracked. Sunlight streams through the edges of the windows,
where the curtains don't reach. I'm gonna have to get those
fixed.

I double check to make sure Luke's fully in the shadows
before I extract myself from his grip and get up. The clock
says noon. Why the hell did I wake up?

Then I hear it again. Pounding. Someone is trying to break
down my door.

I yawn and call out, "Hold on a second!" I stretch. I rub my
neck as I pad to the door. I squeeze outside and shut the
door behind me so Luke can sleep.

"What?"

Flowers stands on my stoop. He's breathing hard, like a bull.
I think he might be about to charge.

"Olé."

He doesn't get my half-awake joke. He starts pacing. "We
have to research everything there is to know about demon
and thae breeds," he says. "I need to know your exact
heritage. We need to spend every goddamn hour thiguring
out—"

"Um, hi. I'm Lyon. You're Diego Flores, my boss."

His eyebrows lower. "You're the worst thing that has ever happened to me."

"Are you on catnip again? You're at my apartment. It's the middle of the day. Why aren't you sleeping?"

Diego's eyes go black and he marches toward me until he looms over me. "I'm not sleeping because your stupid magic didn't just erase a letter."

"What?"

He doesn't respond, just continues to try to burn me to a crisp with his eyes.

It takes a second for my waking brain to connect the dots. I see a big fuchsia stain on his neck before it clicks. But when it does, my jaw goes slack. "Oh. No. You lost your effing…" My stupid magic!!!!

But … how? He didn't have a date for Blue Snow last morning. We arrested Marian at Sue's …

Fuchsia lipstick. He and Sue. He likes the tigress type? Or the mix?

I accidentally picture him as a tiger and the girger getting it on. Then I frantically erase that mental image, like a grade schooler jumping around erasing a white board. No. Nope. No-no-no.

Flowers grits his teeth. His hands curl into fists. He wants to pummel me, I can tell.

"Drink the pee," I tell him. "I even have some in my fridge. Doctor sent it for you. I can grab it."

"There has to be a better way," he argues.

I grab my doorknob. "Don't worry. We'll get your groove back. Light your dynamite. All that jizz."

"Ith you spit out one more erection metaphor, I'm shithting to my tiger and eating you."

"No pooping tigers allowed," I chirp back.

"Thox!"

I sneak inside and fumble around in the fridge. I grab the cup that Brynhildr made me take, grateful that she sent it along. Wise old valkyrie.

I slip back out onto the porch and hand it to Flowers, who wrinkles his nose, unscrews the lid, stares down at the cup in fury.

I feel kinda wrong about it, but a total sense of giddy, hell-yeah muthatrucker vengeance surges through me as Flowers raises that cup.

He downs the nasty dark yellow liquid in one gulp. "Fuck!" he swears.

I gag, imagining the taste. And then groan as I realize I missed my chance. "Aww, I totally should have grabbed my camera!"

"Lyon!" a shrill feminine voice calls up the stairs just as Flowers' hand wraps around my throat.

I think that voice is the only reason Flowers doesn't kill me.

We both turn, my neck still tight in his grip, to see the figure on the stairs. Sparkling orange dress, glinting wings, coiffed hair …Mother Dearest smiles at me.

"I wasn't sure you'd be up. How convenient."

"Hi mom," I say stiffly.

Mom eyes Flowers but just sniffs. She's not a big fan of shifters.

"I left a message, but I'm here to collect you, so I hope you're packed."

"Packed for what?"

She rolls her eyes. "Don't you young people ever listen to those voice recordings? The King of the Summer Court has summoned you beyond the Veil."

A PERSONAL NOTE FROM LYON FOX

Hey there 3rd BFF (you know, after JR and Seena):

How's it hanging? Life good?

The author's totally given me a couple pixie sticks so I'm feeling chill AF right now. She and I have been chatting about when the next book should come out. Personally, I'd rather avoid it. I can't believe she's forcing me to spend time with my mother!

But ultimately, we've decided, when that book gets written is up to you. I mean, if all my books hit 500 reviews, then January 1, she'll start drafting my new adventure. But when the magic happens for me all comes down to you and your magic fingers. (*That's what she said!*—couldn't help myself.) Your reviews trigger the online book store's magical algorithms. And I'm pretty sure we all just learned math is magic. If you need more proof, just look at my bank account, that gold disappears every month! But you have a rare and wondrous ability to make math work for good instead of evil. You have the power to make my stories appear out of thin air and become visible to other readers with your reviews.

Help a fairy out!

Spread the word, mockingbird! Tell a friend about me. Word of mouth is totes important, too. I mean, you know I'm awesome. I know I'm awesome. We just need other people to see how awesome I am so that you and I can hang out more. M'kay, 3rd BFF? (If you help me out and review books 1, 2, 3, and 4, I might consider kicking Seena out of the number two spot and giving it to you.)

Oh, and if you wanna join the author's Facebook group and tell her how much you love me, I see those messages, too. I'd totally love that. Plus, I mean, have you seen the pics she posted of the chickie pups? Totes adorable. Inspiration pics go up there. Updates. Secrets. You know. The good stuff. Maybe if you help me harass her, I'll get books faster!!! It's Ann Denton's Reader Group. See ya in there!

All the hearts—

Ly

AFTERWORD

Thank you so much for reading! You are amazing, and you are the reason I can keep dreaming up beautiful worlds. If you liked this book, please leave a review and tell your friends!

Your reviews and recommendations keep me pumped up as I write the next book. So, thanks!

ACKNOWLEDGMENTS

A huge thanks to Rob, Raven, Ivy, Coralee, Thais, and Mia.

Another HUGE shout-out to all my readers out there. You guys keep me moving and writing! When I see you all chatting about the books in my Facebook group, it totally energizes and encourages me.

OTHER BOOKS BY THE AUTHOR

If you'd like to read my other work, which is more naughty and less "fade to black", but with plenty of witty banter, then feel free to read any of the following series under my other pen name - Ann Denton.

Choose from books on the following pages based on your current reading mood.

The standalone or the first book in each series are listed by mood. The darkest reads appear first and grow progressively more light-hearted so it makes it easy to find just what you're looking for next. I also tried to add some basic mood info at the bottom of each series page for you.

FERAL PRINCESS SERIES
(Completed Trilogy)

A hot, dark shifter omegaverse with dub con, a steamy alpha, a loving beta, and a sassy omega who thought she was going to be an alpha female. She was sooo wrong, but when she's claimed by the pack alpha, make no mistake, she has something to say about it.

Defiant - Book 1

Mood - #DARK #DIRTY #ALPHA

STALKED AND PLUCKED SERIES
(Series of Standalones)

A fast-burn, contemporary MF romance series with very morally gray men who stalk their ladies before claiming them. The series follows a group of college girls who are best friends.

Chaining Daisy - Book 1

Mood - #HOT #HOLYHELL #NEWKINKUNLOCKED

PINNACLE SERIES
(Completed Duet)

A medium-burn paranormal romance about a girl who gets herself sent to a reform academy on purpose, so she can recruit criminally-minded guys to pull off the magical heist of the century. (Reverse Harem)

Magical Academy for Delinquents #MAD - Book 1

Mood - #BADASS #FUN #SEXY GAMES

TANGLED CROWNS SERIES
(Completed Trilogy and spinoff in progress)

A medium-burn, medieval fantasy romance with a reluctant princess, the knights she jilted at the alter, and an enemies to lovers story that weaves laughter and tears together along with a plot to save the kingdom. (Reverse Harem)

Knightfall - Book 1

Mood - #BANTER #REDEMPTION #WHAATJUSTHAPPENED

LOTTO LOVE SERIES
(Completed Duet)

A medium-burn, contemporary romantic comedy reverse harem about winning the lotto and doing whatever the hell you want with it, even if that means holding a Bachelorette-style competition for an entire harem of hotties.

Lotto Men - Book 1

Mood- #LOL #BLUSHING #NO WAY

RUBY - JEWELS CAFE SERIES
(Standalone)

A medium-burn, fated mates reverse harem with an angel on her last strike, some nerds and a tech demon determined to help her, and Christmas miracles.

Ruby

Mood - #SWEET #AWWW #GIGGLES

DARK TEMPTATIONS SERIES
(Incomplete)

A fast-burn monster reverse harem in an alternate reality where monsters rule the earth. A human woman is captured and auctioned off to the Four Terrors who will haunt her nightmares and her dreams alike.
Cowrite with Katie May.

Ravaged by Monsters - Book 1

Mood - #DARK #FATED LOVE #WILD SEXY TIMES

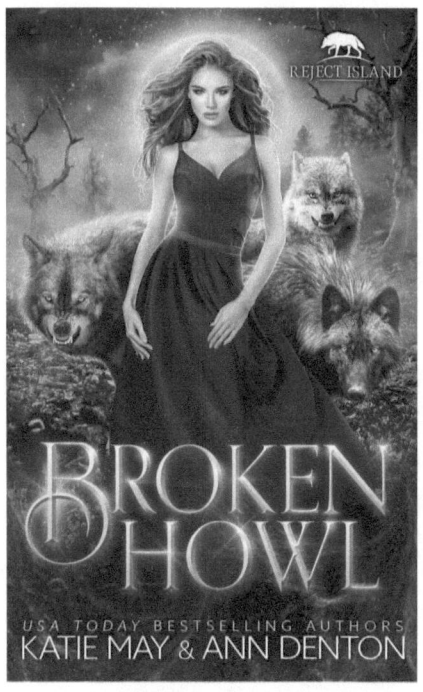

BROKEN HOWL

(Standalone)

A female omega rejects her mates so she can escape her
abuser. She's sent to an island for rejects but her mates refuse
to let her go...
Cowrite with Katie May.

Broken Howl

Mood - #CRYING #HEALING #FIGHTING

Darkest Queen Series
(Incomplete)

The devil is a woman. And this is the story about she fell from Heaven only to rise as God's greatest enemy... (A reverse harem spinoff of the Darkest Flames series) Cowrite with Katie May.

For Whom the Bell Tolls - Book 1

Mood - #FURY #SOUL-DEEP CONNECTIONS #BATTLE OF WILLS

DARKEST FLAMES SERIES
(Completed Trilogy with a novella)

A medium-burn paranormal romance about a girl who tries
a love spell on the hot guy at school and accidentally
summons demons instead. It contains psychotic, alpha
males, and student/teacher relationships. (Reverse Harem)
Cowrite with Katie May.

Demon Kissed - Book 1

Mood - #OOPS #NAUGHTY LAUGHTER #FORBIDDEN HEAT

Demon's Joy
(Standalone)

Santa's daughter has to save Christmas from demons! And all she's got to help her are five funny reindeer. (A reverse harem spinoff of the Darkest Flames series) Cowrite with Katie May.

Demon's Joy

Mood - #SILLY #HOLIDAY CHEER #YUM

MAGE SHIFTER WAR SERIES
(Completed Duet)

A medium-burn paranormal mafia romance. A fae princess is taken captive by three shifter criminals. (Reverse Harem) Cowritten with Elle Middaugh.

Fae Captive - Book 1

Mood - #BONNIE&CLYDE #BADASS #HOT

HAMMER TIME
(Standalone)

A medium-burn paranormal comedy featuring Thor's daughter and a quest to save demigods from prison. Expect lots of ancient deities and potty humor. (Reverse Harem) Cowritten with M.J. Marstens.

Hammer Time

Mood- #PUNTASTIC #NOYOUDIDN'T #SNORT

CONNECT AND GET SNEAK PEEKS

If you like to read exclusive snippets from different characters, make predictions with other readers, see my inspiration for books, or just come hang and be yourself, I have a Facebook reader group.

Go Here to Join Ann Denton's Reader Group:

https://www.facebook.com/AuthorAnnaDare

ABOUT ME

I'm a Virgo. I've driven around town finding landmarks based on a friend's dream. And, I'm addicted to dark chocolate bars with espresso. I have a hubster who encourages my crazy pants ways. I have two amazing little humans who look up to me right now, but won't for long because I'm very short.

I love the arts: painting, theatre, and reading. I have an undergrad degree in Playwriting and a grad degree in Theatre History. Socrates rocks my socks.

I'm an INTJ. If you've never taken a Meyers Briggs personality test, I recommend them.

I would love to talk to you about the book. Yes you. You can ask me questions on Facebook. If you sign up for my newsletter on my website, I'll email you about upcoming books.

Anna@AuthorAnnaDare.com

www.AuthorAnnaDare.com